TEASE ME

TEASE ME

A collection of twenty erotic stories

Edited by Miranda Forbes

Published by Accent Press Ltd – 2008
ISBN 9781906125844

Printed and bound in the UK

Cover Design by
Red Dot Design

Contents

The First Time – The Last Time   Sally Quilford   1

The 'What-If' Monster   Jade Taylor   10

Skin Deep   Cathryn Cooper   19

Strangers On A Bus   Nicky B   28

Keeping It Real   Landon Dixon   34

The Fitting Room   Roger Frank Selby   45

My Immortal   Sally Quilford   60

Ladies' Circle   Kaycie Wolfe   68

Begging For It   Emily Dubberley   83

Lorelei's Day Of Play   Chloe Devlin   90

New Boots   Carmel Lockyer   102

On The Carpet   Cathy King   109

Pants On Fire   Sommer Marsden   118

Canadian Postcard   Lynn Lake   125

Spanked To Her Senses   Jim Baker   131

Two Of A Kind   J. Manx   142

Bathing Minerva   Jeremy Edwards   153

Darling   Sommer Marsden   161

Birthday Blues   Judith Roycroft   168

Railway Signals   J. Manx   180

The First Time - The Last Time
by Sally Quilford

The first time we started in the lift on the way to your apartment. Lips met and tongues collided, tasted, demanded. Your mouth found my throat, moving lower. Over your shoulder I could see us reflected in the mirror, and we seemed to be another couple. Not the shy English woman with the bold American, who'd met at a party and were only planning a no-strings one-night stand, but a couple who were meant to stay together for life.

I'd seen you across the room at the party and thought if you didn't come and speak to me by the time I'd finished my first drink, you never would. Then if you didn't come and speak to me by the time I'd finished my second drink, you never would. After my third drink, terrified that you wouldn't speak to me, and emboldened by the liquor, I walked over and invited you to dance.

'I thought you'd never ask,' you said. I wondered if you'd ever had to do the running where women were concerned.

I swayed against you, the alcohol making my head swim. You held me close, but not too close, and to onlookers we probably looked very formal, but your eyes – those dark brown eyes that burned with intensity – were locked on mine, and your hands – those hands with

1

their long, slender fingers which learned how to reach every part of me – your hands felt hot through my thin blouse. I had to hide my face in your shoulder, unable to stand the intensity of your eyes. That only weakened my resolve, as I breathed in your animal scent, mixed with the subtle cologne I imagined you rubbing onto your body after you'd stepped from the shower. I knew you for less than five minutes and already I was imagining your naked body stepping out of the shower, rivulets running down your chest, into a thick line of hair below your navel, then downwards, into a thick mass of hair.

'What are you thinking?' you asked.

'Nothing.'

'Oh.'

'Well, I'm just thinking that this is nice. Dancing with you.' And seeing you get out of the shower would be nice too, I thought, as the image filled my head again.

'I was hoping that you were imagining how it would be if you and I made love.' From any other man it would have sounded perverted and presumptuous. In your deep, rich voice it was the most sensual thing I'd ever heard. My body tingled against yours. 'Come home with me, Gina,' you whispered against my lips, your tongue lightly touching the corner of my mouth.

It was one of those moments at a crossroads. Did I pretend to be something I wasn't and go with you for one night? Or did I keep my dignity and tell you thanks but no thanks? I tried to refuse. I wanted to talk to you first. Get to know you. Have dinner. Go on a few dates. I protested just long enough to let you know that I was usually a good girl. As you drew me closer still, I began to forget that girl. Forget that I was the type who slept with a man only if I was in love with him. The sort of girl who once she'd slept with a man did fall in love with

2

him. Once you'd taken me to your bed, you couldn't trust me not to want to stay with you for ever but how could I have told you that when we'd only just met? It was too complicated, and you'd have walked out of my life, leaving me with yet another missed chance. So I let you take my hand and lead me from the party.

We stumbled out of the lift at your floor, giggling. You dragged me by the hand to your apartment and I was reminded of a caveman pulling his chosen woman by the hair. I'd have let you do that too if you'd wanted to.

We fell through your apartment door and, when you shut it, you slammed me against the wall, displacing a bit of the plaster, which fell to the floor behind me. Your hands lifted my skirt, while we kissed and I tore at your shirt, revealing your chest. I ran my nails through the fine dark hair, lightly scratching your nipples, and bending my head to flick them with my tongue. I opened the zipper on your trousers, sliding my hands in to find your burgeoning erection and free it from its confines. Your breath was hot on my neck, and when I ran my hands along your length, you let out a low growl, biting into the skin along my collarbone. Frantic hands tore at my panties, pulling them aside and parting me with hot fingertips. My body wanted you so badly that my vulva, desperate for relief, almost sucked your fingers inwards, my body sliding down onto them, deeper and deeper until I could hardly breathe for excitement.

You sank to the ground, pulling my panties down over my feet as you descended, then parting my thighs before sinking your face into my sex, breathing me in. Your fingers sank deep into me again, while your tongue found my clit, teasing me, sucking it into your mouth, fingers and tongue probing, while my body responded with a rhythmic throbbing. I raised one leg to give you more

3

room to taste me, reaching out, needing something to hold onto, one hand on the wall above me, and the other in your thick curls, pulling your head into me.

When I came, shuddering against you, you lay back on the floor, your erection pointing to the ceiling.

'My turn?'

For a brief moment I remembered myself, which was a shame, as I'd wanted so much to forget.

'OK,' I whispered, falling to my knees. 'But don't come in my mouth.' I wanted to kick myself the moment I said it. You just laughed and promised not to. For a long time afterwards you teased me about it, and though you never said it, I knew other women let you. But I wanted to please you as much as I could within my own limits, so after slowly and seductively taking off my blouse and bra, so you could look at me, I wanted you to look at me – to see something in me that you'd want to spend your life with – I kneeled over you and teased the damp tip of your cock with my tongue, taking you into my mouth, then letting it slide out again, giggling when it bobbed away from me. At the same time I cupped your scrotum in my hands, squeezing, kneading.

You growled, gripping your own hair with one hand, your head tilted back in ecstasy. Your other hand moved to my head, and when I wrapped my lips around you again, you pushed my head down, so that the tip slid to the back of my mouth. It aroused me more than I imagined it could, so I sucked harder, dragging my teeth gently along its length, while you groaned and writhed upwards. You pulled the bottom half of my body around to you, putting my legs either side of your head, and we lay in the sixty-nine position, you fingering and licking me, while I sucked you. Just the thought of being in a position I'd once considered dirty aroused me beyond measure. I felt wanton and wicked, and loved every minute of it, grinding my hips back against you, whilst taking you deep into my mouth.

Feeling you were on the verge of coming, and unable to get past that last taboo I'd set for myself, I stopped and was about to sit astride you, when you helped me to my feet, and bent me over the back of a chair. Your fingers trailed my bare back, and then you slid my skirt upwards, exposing my buttocks, which you covered with gentle kisses. I felt your hands curl around my thighs, while your thumbs slipped into me, then out, spreading the moisture to my thighs. I wanted your tongue again and waited. Instead I felt you stand up straight and the tip of your rock hard cock teased my vulva, promising the pleasure soon to come.

'Oh please,' I said, licking my lips. 'Please.'

You teased me for a little while longer, stroking my labia with your cock, while I wriggled back against you, wanting every inch of you inside me. In one hard thrust you were, almost forcing me over the back of the chair. We laughed – we used to laugh a lot then, remember? Our laughter was soon replaced by moans of pleasure as one thrust was followed by another, and you ground deep into me, slamming your thighs against mine, while your mouth covered my back with kisses and love bites. It was all I could do to keep hold of the chair, while wave after wave of pleasure crashed over my body. I never knew that sex could be so animal, so bruising and so ecstatic. When we came together, I sobbed with the intensity of it all, feeling strangely sad in the knowledge that this was going to be the most intense sex I'd ever have.

You turned me around and held me in your arms, stroking my hair and kissing my cheek. 'Did I hurt you?'

I couldn't explain that the pain wasn't physical, and

neither were the tears all of sadness. You may never know how many boundaries I crossed for you that night, partly to keep you and partly because it felt all right when I was with you. I gave you more of myself than I'd ever given any man. You left me not only physically naked, but psychologically laid bare. You took me to your bed where you held me close and then made love to me with such tenderness it was all I could do not to cry again.

We lasted beyond that first night. At least as long as I remained working in America. People said we were good together. Other women – those who wanted you as much as I did – hated me. Other men seemed to find me more attractive and I turned down more offers than I'd had in my whole adult life.

Then came time for me to return home. I waited for you to ask me to stay. To offer marriage, or simply to suggest I ask my firm to extend my contract. Surely after all we'd shared, in bed and out of it, you'd want me to stay? I was afraid to suggest it in case I forced you into a decision. After all, we were only ever intended to be a one-night stand.

On my last night we made our way up in the lift just like the first time. In the reflection in the mirror we looked like two strangers who'd met for a one-night stand and were now wondering how to say goodbye with dignity and without having to leave a forwarding address. I thought I might kiss you, to see if you responded, but your preoccupation with your sneakers forbade it. Someone got into the lift – the same man who got in on our first night – and he looks just as uncomfortable to be there as we are.

We ate dinner and watched the news. People were dying in the world and I wanted to care about them, but how could I when I'd have to leave you tomorrow? They

6

were discussing the next election but what did it matter to me who runs America when I've gone? According to the weather forecast a blizzard was coming, but I'll be gone before it starts so I didn't even bother to warn you to put the snow chains on the car. Little by little the pieces of my life with you were being chipped away and I looked to you for the glue to bind it all together again, but you were too interested in a precipitation that was building over the west coast and that has even less to do with me than the local forecast.

I packed my clothes, still waiting to see if you'd ask me to stay. It was a glitch in our relationship, that was all. At any moment you'd come to the bedroom and beg me not to leave. Then I told myself that if you didn't come into the bedroom to ask me to stay by the time I zipped up my case, you weren't going to ask me.

I sat on the bed when I'd finished packing, still convinced you'd be along any minute. Instead you stayed in the lounge, drinking whisky and watching the late news. Then when my case was zipped, I told myself it would be like the films, where you rushed to the airport at the last minute and boarded the plane to serenade me with our song. There was plenty of time. And then there was no time. It was gone midnight and today was the day I was going to leave you forever.

I took my courage, of which there was very little, into my hands and went to find you.

'Hello. Got any more whisky?'

'Yep, here.' You handed me the bottle and I took a swig straight from it. 'You finished packing?'

I struggled to see if your indifference was feigned, but it was always hard to tell with you. I sat astride you and kissed you long and hard. Did I imagine that you weren't returning it with the same gusto as the first night?

'For old time's sake,' I said, slipping my hands into your shirt.

'Sure. Why not?'

I kissed you again, trying not to cry, trying not to admit to myself that I never was meant to be the sort of woman to interest you for ever. Perhaps it was too late, but I thought I might have one last chance. Slipping down onto my knees, I unzipped your jeans and pulled down your boxers, revealing your cock. Six months earlier and it would have been already erect. I put my head down and took you into my mouth. Then you became hard, unable to stem the natural instinct, and your hand softly stroked my hair. I missed the urgency with which you'd slammed my head down on that first night. I don't know if you felt my tears fall onto your belly. I was too busy proving my point, taking you deep into my mouth. I felt you twitch, and you were going to pull away – I'd trained you that well – but I kept you there, sucking you hard, while my hands encircled the base of your cock, sliding upwards, drawing you to my mouth. The pressure of your hand increased on the back of my head, and finally you came.

I looked up at you, and for an instant I thought your eyes were sad, but when you saw me looking that was quickly replaced with a smile and a quiet, 'Wow.'

Afterwards you carried me to bed, and we lay together in the silence, my head on your chest. I thought of how trivial the whole thing had been, worrying about how it would taste and feel if I let you come into my mouth. Then I realised that because it was so trivial, it changed nothing. Even if I'd let you do it that first night. After all, the other women who let you weren't with you now.

Sometime during the long sleepless night, you went down on me, bringing me to a climax languidly. As if we had all the time in the world. As if it wouldn't be the last time. It was my consolation prize for being a good girl, I think.

I slept at last, but when I awoke you'd gone. I phoned the taxi and drove to the airport, arriving at ten o'clock for my noon flight. Sitting there with a cappuccino, listening to Luther on my Ipod and wondering if you'd notice my empty chair, I told myself that if you didn't arrive by ten-thirty you weren't coming. Flights came and left. If you didn't arrive by eleven you weren't coming. Families parted, lovers reunited. If you didn't arrive by eleven-thirty you weren't coming. My flight was called. If you didn't arrive by the time I got to the departure gate you weren't coming …

As I took out my boarding pass, resigned to walking away from you for ever, my cell phone bleeped to tell me I'd got a message.

'Pls wait. I'm coming to bring you back home. I love you.'

The 'What-If' Monster
by Jade Taylor

I could lie, and say it wasn't jealousy.

That after too many bad relationships to count, that after everything that had happened, that my securities were finally over.

That marriage meant trust.

And logically, coolly and calmly, I did trust him.

But sometimes logic had nothing to do with it.

Logic couldn't calm the 'what-if' monster.

What if he was drunk?

What if he was having doubts?

What if his mates pressured him into doing something stupid?

What if the strippers were prettier, sexier, *better* than me?

When we'd discussed his stag do I'd been fine about the idea, now the 'what-if' monster was going mad in my head.

I was out dancing with my friends – not at the hen party, that had been a fortnight ago – in a gay bar where he didn't have anything for the 'what-if' monster to bother him with.

No, this was our not-the-stag-do, my friends' husbands and boyfriends were out with my fiancée, and we hadn't wanted to all wait at home for them while they were up to mischief.

Occasionally you'd see my friends check their mobiles, checking for texts they wouldn't have heard over the blaring music, wondering what their partners were up to.

I wondered if the 'what-if' monster was bothering them, too.

So maybe it wasn't a good idea to crash the stag do. By that point we'd had the rudely named cocktails, the cheap shots, the strange concoctions, and none of us was exactly thinking clearly, least of all me.

But the 'what-if' monster was calling, asking what if you checked up on him? He's only the other side of town and if you did maybe you'd get a good night's sleep and stop stressing.

Or maybe you'd find out he was just like the others.

And what if he was?

It was one 'what if' too many.

I stagger over to my Kate, my best mate.

'I'm going to call it a night, I'm knackered, and at least one of us should be in a fit state to find the paracetamol tomorrow.'

'Don't be such a wimp,' she moans. 'He won't be home for hours yet, stay a bit longer.'

I shake my head firmly. 'No Kate, I'm going to make tracks.' I lean over to kiss her cheek. 'Text me in the morning.'

I ignore the others' cat-calls of cowardice as I leave.

As the cold air hits me I should feel the alcohol hit too, should feel too drunk for daft scheming, should decide a better idea would be to drink two glasses of water and sleep it off.

Instead I feel as if the cold air has helped clear my

11

mind, has made my mad idea seem suddenly like nothing more than common sense. I lift my arm to hail a taxi.

Josh, Liam's best mate and best man sees me almost as soon as I walk in. I stuck out like a sore thumb; the only woman in there wearing clothes.

To be fair to Josh, he does a good job of trying to stop me. Although he can hardly stand he manages to weave his way over to me and tell me that this isn't a good idea.

As if I hadn't already thought that (and then promptly discarded that thought).

'Jo, you shouldn't be here!' He smiles as he says it, laughing like it's all just another fun part of the evening, but there's fear in his eyes; I know his wife.

'I just thought I'd see what you boys were up to.'

I look around the room; most of the boys are sitting slack-jawed in front of the main stage where a dancer is demonstrating her flexibility, struck dumb with either lust or alcohol or a potent combination of both. A few are standing at the bar, mainly the older and married men, drinking as if it's the only thing they're permitted to do while occasionally sneaking furtive looks back at the stage. A few of the group are missing.

Liam is missing.

I turn my attention back to Josh.

'Where's Liam?'

He's too drunk to think of a convincing lie; instead he pauses too long, and comes up with, 'He popped out to get a breath of fresh air.'

That line worked so much better before the smoking ban kicked in.

'Wouldn't I have seen him on the way in?' I ask.

Again a long pause.

'He's out the back. The smoking bit.' He pauses

again, maybe realising that 'the smoking bit' doesn't exactly provide fresh air. He shifts from foot to foot (why do men look like kids who need to pee when they're caught lying?), then his face lights up as he realises something he obviously thinks is brilliant.

'He went to phone you.'

A brilliant line, if not so easily checkable.

I ferret my mobile out of handbag. 'No missed calls.'

'Maybe he's not rung you yet.' He stares at the phone, willing it to ring.

It doesn't.

I head for the stage, aiming for one of the drunkest blokes.

'Where's Liam?'

'Back room, getting a private dance,' he replies, so fixated on the blonde on stage he doesn't even turn around to see who's asking.

I head for the back rooms.

Now I never knew they had bouncers at strip clubs. Thinking about it, it obviously makes sense, but in my inebriated state I'd just thought I'd breeze through.

Good job the man mountain there was blessed with brawn and not brains.

Ducking into the shadows I quickly reapply lip gloss and hoick my boobs up even further than the Wonderbra already had.

'I'm looking for the stag,' I giggle flirtatiously. 'I'm a surprise.'

'Last door on the left with Jenna,' he tells me, waving me through to the private rooms, slapping my arse as I go by.

I open the door quietly, intending to sneak inside, but there's no need for sneaking; nobody's looking at me.

Instead in the darkness Liam is sprawled on a couch,

13

watching the mini-stage where the spotlight focuses on the dancing blonde.

She wasn't pretty.

Her nose was too long, her eyes too wide-set, her blonde hair just slightly too brassy for her skin tone. Her body was good, but not amazing; obviously once she'd obsessively worked out at the gym but had let it slide. But it didn't matter.

She was sexy as hell – and Liam wanted her.

I watched as he spread his legs further apart, as if his balls were suddenly the size of basketballs when I knew they were nothing more than average, shifting in his seat to hide his erection.

I could see why she was having such an effect.

She's already stripped down to her bra and thong, and as her hips sway in time to the music I know that although I could easily (and happily) list her imperfections she's so confident in her sexuality they're all irrelevant.

I pause, ready to lose my temper. Liam and I had discussed tonight, and though I'd been happy for him to go to a strip club, I'd said that I didn't want him having a private dance.

And he'd agreed.

So what had changed?

I'm so ready to start shouting, to start becoming the shrew his friends no doubt expect I'll become before the ink's even dry on our marriage certificate, when she sees me.

And I think, what if I don't do that?

What if, instead of turning into a screaming harridan, I join in? What if I make *myself* part of this fantasy?

I smile at her.

She smiles back.

'Shit, Jo, what are you doing here?' He stumbles to his feet, his erection wilting before my eyes. 'It's not what you think.'

'Oh, I'm pretty sure it is,' I tell him, but I'm smiling as I walk over and put my hand on his chest to push him back down. 'Now why don't you relax?'

He's confused, I can see, but the dancer, Jenna, has caught on, and winks at me as she turns to give me a hand up on to the small stage.

I've never done this before, and though I've faked flirting with my girlfriends before to get boys' attention, I'm nervous as I step closer.

She's not.

Her hands go to my hips to pull me closer, to move me in time to the music, and I start to relax, telling myself it's only dancing.

It's only dancing.

As she moves her hands higher, up over my waist, I hear him breathe in sharply, then groan as her hands cup my breasts. I close my eyes, still moving to the music, still telling myself to relax as she slowly circles her thumbs around my nipples. They harden and I'm sure she can feel that I'm bra-less.

I step closer and open my eyes.

She's sexy as hell, and knowing that Liam is watching, that this is turning him on is making me so wet.

She's smiling as she moves her hands to my butt, caressing it softly before sharply pulling me forward.

She pushes up my skirt slightly so her leg can go between mine, so our dancing turns to grinding as she rubs herself against me. I can't help but follow.

I turn to look at Liam, and watch as he strokes his cock through his jeans.

15

I can read his mind, see how he wants me to kiss her. So I do.

I turn back to her and slowly lick my lips, knowing that she's watching me, wondering how far I'm going to take this. I can see from her half-closed eyes and dilated pupils that she's not faking this arousal, that she's enjoying this as much as I am.

Her mouth tastes sweet, like cherry lip-gloss, and though at first I'm all nerves and hesitancy I'm soon kissing her hard, tongues meeting as our bodies get closer. My hands go to her breasts, squeezing them gently then teasing her hardening nipples.

Fuck, I've never felt so turned on before, and can't believe it's from kissing a woman in a seedy club while my fiancée watches.

Then all thoughts are lost as she reaches behind her to remove her bra, then reaches for my top and quickly pulls it off.

Now as we kiss I can feel her breasts rubbing against me, her nipples stroking me, my nipples rubbing against her as our tongues continue to tease each other.

I'm rubbing myself against her thigh and can feel how wet I am, how close I am to coming.

I force myself to break away, knowing that although this is giving Liam a great private show, I can make it better.

I hook my thumbs around Jenna's thong.

'We'll take off our panties if you take your boxers down.'

Liam doesn't pause for a second, quickly standing to pull down his jeans and boxers and sits down bare-arsed, clothing bundled around his ankles while his hard-on bobs around demanding attention.

The tip is already slick with pre-cum, and I watch as

his thumb rubs the moisture around his cock, so when he grips it again his hand slides up and down more easily.

I've never seen him wanking before, and now the sight of it is wonderfully erotic.

I'm so distracted by it I'm still until he prompts, 'I've kept my part of the deal,' in a husky voice.

I reach for Jenna's thong, quickly pulling it down, smelling the muskiness of her arousal.

I slide my hand between her legs, she's so slick and ready, and it just turns me on more.

She pulls down my skirt and panties and then pulls me down to lie of the floor of the stage with her.

It's cold, but I don't care as I kiss her again, heat flooding through my body. Her tongue is in my mouth and her hand is between my legs and as she teases my clit with her quick fingers I open my legs further, knowing I'm giving Liam a fantastic view. I move so I can touch her, so I can slide my fingers against her swollen clit, and as I do see my future husband's hand moving faster and faster, fisting his cock furiously.

I kiss Jenna again, then lie back as she kisses my breasts, all the time stroking her clit while she strokes mine.

Then she moves to kiss me again and I hear her breathing faster, the little sighs she makes as she clasps her thighs hard around my hand as the pulses consume her. That's all it takes to make me come, and as I do so I can hear Liam crying out, and knowing he's coming too makes my orgasm longer and stronger.

Afterwards it should be awkward, but it's not; we laugh and joke as Jenna passes around her handy box of tissues, and I tell Liam to make sure he tips her well.

We walk out of the room slightly dishevelled, sweaty and smelling of sex, but when Liam's friends turn to look he holds my hand and tells them, 'I'm the luckiest man in the world!'

God knows what they make of that; hopefully they're too drunk to figure it all out, but I know that I don't have to worry about them thinking I'm a nagging shrew any more when they holler and yell enthusiastically.

'Perhaps we could do that again some time,' Liam suggests optimistically as we finally cuddle up in bed.

'Maybe,' I tell him, because you never know.

Because what if I want to?

Skin Deep
by Cathryn Cooper

The boy was beautiful. He'd come to stay at the insistence of a relative.

'Francis needs somewhere to stay – it'll only be for a while. Besides, it will do you good. Make you behave yourself instead of using these women the way you do.'

His aunt had been insistent. She was old and wealthy and he had no intention of upsetting her.

She was right of course; he did treat women badly. He expected and got total submission. They'd nibble his toenails if he asked them to. He was handsome, rich and never lacking for female company – physical contact only. Nothing emotional. He preferred variety for the sort of sex he enjoyed.

The boy was an encumbrance he would learn to live with. Shut him away in a room in the east wing, and that would be that. Or so he thought.

The boy, a lad of not much more than sixteen it seemed, had other ideas. Everywhere Carew went, Francis was there at his elbow.

At first it annoyed him, but over a period of weeks something happened: for a start he registered just how attractive the boy was. His hair was dark blond, soft and silky, falling over his temple in a gentle wave. His eyes were of the rarest blue and fringed with dark lashes. His lips held the sensuous lines of a courtesan, full, wide and the colour of crushed rose petals.

In the beginning he had sought to escape the boy's company, but as time went on he found, much to his unease, that he sought the boy out, missing him when he wasn't around. And that smile! That soft hand easing into his, the round bottom, the hairless chin and even the scent of the lad were intoxicating.

At night he dreamed: wet dreams that he'd been inserting his cock between boyish cheeks, kissing that sweet, girlish mouth. His desires sickened but also tantalized.

His friends began to notice.

'Are you turning the *other* way?' asked one of his friends. 'It's been noticed that you're spending more time with the lad than with the ladies.'

Carew fixed him with an icy glare. 'How would you like your nose rearranged?'

The friend had laughed and pretended it was all just a joke, but Carew knew it wasn't. They had noticed his behaviour and losing face worried him. His reputation of super-stud was at risk. It embarrassed him. He had to do something about it.

Priscilla Palmer-Tovey arrived at Thompson Towers on the dot of seven. Like any parson's daughter, Prissy was polite, punctual and, although not exactly plain, she wasn't beautiful either. Carew watched her walk up the drive, straighten her hat and smooth her dress before she rang the bell. Priscilla was neat in dress but not prim when she was out of it, and at times that suited him very well indeed.

He smiled and drained the lingering dregs of whisky from his glass.

20

There followed a gentle knock on the door to his private sitting room, which was on the first floor and had high lead-paned windows and wainscot panelling. Imran, his servant, entered, bowing before making his announcement.

'Miss Priscilla Palmer-Tovey, sir.'

'As her to come up – and Imran ...'

'Tell Master Francis that I wish to see him.'

'Yes, sir.'

He poured himself another drink to help drown the confusion deep in his groin. He loved women. He knew he did, so why did the boy unnerve him so much and make him think otherwise?

'Don't worry, old chap,' he muttered to himself. 'With Priscilla's assistance, it will be confirmed before the boy's very eyes. He'll not mistake your meaning, old boy. He'll get the message that you want no more of those doe eyes and come-on looks. Good God, didn't you leave all that behind you at boarding school?' A peel of laughter preceded Priscilla's entrance. She rushed into his arms, her face flushed and hot beneath his lips.

'Darling, Roo,' she gushed, her eyes as bright as a child's on Christmas morning. 'How marvellous it is to see you again.'

She smelt of lavender and cabbage roses and her dress seemed a mixed bag of the same – pretty, floral and as busy as a cottage garden.

He smiled. 'Prissy. It's nice to see you, too. I'm really glad you could come.'

Prissy's eyebrows rose. She looked surprised. 'Why, darling Roo. How kind of you. I've never heard you say that to me before.'

Now, thought Carew, I've truly spoken out of character. I never tell her it's nice to see her. Will she

21

suspect I have a specific purpose in mind – a more urgent purpose than usual?

He smiled casually into the round face, the pale eyes and freckled nose. No, he decided, Prissy would not suspect. Like a hungry cat, she would lap up any titbit of affection he threw her and, as always, she would be malleable to his wishes.

He made an effort to control his body and make it as it always was when she appeared – rigid, unbending. All the moves were hers, all the pleasure would be his.

She ran her hands over him, her breath coming in quick, short gasps as she explored his haired chest, his tight stomach and the hot mound in his trousers. Her hand was still rolling over it when Imran returned.

Francis, eyes downcast, was right behind him. Immediately on his entering the room, something stirred beneath the hand of the parson's daughter. Carew was very aware of it. So was Priscilla. Her eyes opened very wide. With a tremendous surge of willpower, Carew reverted to polite protocol in order to disguise Francis's effect on him.

'Ah, Francis. I have someone here I would like you to meet.'

He spoke stiffly, moving his body away from the touch of Prissy's hand.

Priscilla greed Francis politely, but Carew wanted more. Grasping her shoulders he nudged her forward.

'Don't you think Francis is a good-looking young man?'

'Yes.'

'But he's shy,' said Carew, 'and you, my darling Prissy, are going to help him get over his shyness. We're going to show him something that will warm his blood. I guarantee he'll never be shy again – especially with women.'

In response to his fingers, Prissy's nipple pushed against the bodice of her dress.

Carew ordered the boy to sit and watch. Without being ordered, Imran came forward and stood beside the brown leather chair in which Carew sat.

He smiled at Priscilla. 'Well, my dear Prissy, let us show this virgin youth exactly what a woman can do for a man, and exactly what a man can do for a woman.'

With an ecstatic expression on her face, Prissy dropped to her knees between Carew's legs and began undoing her dress buttons. Generous breasts begged for release against the confining pinkness of her bra. Pushing the cups down, she brought out first one breast then the other, the nipples as big as cherries.

Priscilla's breasts disappeared between Carew's knees as she leaned forward, her hands clasping the arms of his chair. With admirable dexterity, she undid his trouser zip with her teeth.

Carew glanced at Francis. The boy was bug-eyed; no doubt he'd be playing with himself given half a chance – that is if he were inclined towards women, something Carew was not at all sure of.

He gave Imran the nod. As Priscilla snuffled to get his cock into her mouth, Imran's brown hands bound her wrists to the chair arms with what looked to be leather dog collars.

Priscilla was positively guzzling at his erection, licking the end, tickling the opening with the tip of her tongue.

Carew threw back his head and moaned in satisfaction. Wondering whether the boy was having an erection, he looked over at Francis and met his eyes, saw the flush of his cheeks and wondered anew …

Another nod from him and Imran lifted Priscilla's skirt, folded it around her waist and pulled down her knickers.

Priscilla squealed as Imran guided his firm, brown rod into the folded crescent of flesh poking out from beneath her thighs.

'In,' said Carew, his voice steady despite his fast breathing. 'Out,' he said.

So directed, Imran thrust and repeated on demand.

'Is she very wet?' he asked.

Imran nodded.

'She's aching for it. But you're not having it all yet, Prissy. Not until you take more of my cock into your throat. Do you understand?'

Prissy understood alright. He knew her well. Knew what she liked and what she was capable of.

With both hands, he manipulated Prissy's head so that her movements were suited to his pleasure. As he did so his eyes never left the face of the boy he knew as Francis.

'Now,' he said to Imran. 'Give it her hard NOW!'

As Imran increased the speed of his thrusts, Carew pressed Priscilla's head more firmly into his lap. 'Suck! Suck me dry!'

He turned to Francis. 'Go on boy. Feel her. Press your hand between her legs and she'll come. Go on. Now!'

Francis stared round-eyed but did nothing.

Carew was furious. The moment he had withdrawn from Priscilla's mouth, he zipped up his fly, leaving Imran to unbuckle the woman from the chair arms.

'Get out,' he said to both of them. 'I want to speak to Francis alone.'

'You disobeyed me. Why was that?'

The boy's cheeks were pink with embarrassment. His eyes glistened as though the shocked stare was there to

24

stay.

'I ...' he began, then swallowed. 'I didn't want to. Not with her.' And then that smile again.

With me! That's what he means! With me!

'That is that!' shouted Carew, his emotions in more disarray than his clothes. 'You've tried my patience enough. It's time you learned not to be so provocative towards me. I won't have it. Do you hear me? I won't have it!'

Francis rose slowly from the chair. 'I'm sorry. I didn't mean ...'

'You didn't mean! You didn't mean!'

This was all too much. He couldn't go on feeling like this. It had to be thrashed out of the boy physically. There was no alternative, not if he was to keep his own sanity.

Before the boy could make a run for it, he grabbed his wrists, yanked him to his feet and dragged him over to the window. The curtains were held back with multi-coloured ropes; he used one of these to bind the boy's wrists together. He threw the end over the overhead rail and tied it firmly in place. He tied him facing the window, anything rather than have those blue eyes beseeching him to desist.

'Please, sir ...' pleaded Francis.

Carew heard him, but something about the boy's tone did not ring true. He couldn't help but get the impression that the boy was pleading for more, not to be released.

Carew clenched his jaw in anger. This confusion, he'd endured; this pain of enticement to an act unnatural to his true nature. The lad was infuriating! So he thought this would be pleasurable did he?

Smiling, he took a bundle of ornamental twigs from a tall urn and bound them together with sticky tape. The tape gave him an idea.

25

'Sir, are you really going to …'

Before Francis could say anything further, before the melodic voice and the big blue eyes could get under his skin, Carew placed a length of tape over the soft pink lips. He considered the eyes too, but thought better of it. It was the boy's voice that got to him.

'I'll teach you,' he said, as much to himself as to the boy.

His hands trembled as he undid the boy's trousers and pulled them down. The smell of youthful flesh resurrected his flagging penis. He slapped at it, thinking it would go down. It didn't.

Fixing his gaze on the plump, round bottom, he reached for the bundle of twigs.

Concentrate. Don't look at his loins.

The twigs made a whooshing sound as they flew through the air. Francis jerked as they landed across the smooth flesh.

Carew didn't stop but raised them for a second, a third and a fourth time. Not until he'd landed six strokes did he pause to study his handiwork. What had been white flesh was now criss-crossed with pink stripes. With trembling fingers he touched what he would once have regarded as taboo territory. The flesh was so soft, so beautiful. He had a terrible urge to release his swollen member, perhaps running it between the lovely cheeks.

He groaned and closed his eyes. His worst nightmare! He desired a boy!

When he opened them again, his eyes strayed to Francis's reflection in the window. No tear escaped the clear blue eyes. The boy did not struggle but eyed him expectantly.

As though he knows I cannot resist.

He allowed his hand to touch the silken hip; he

frowned. Surely it curved like a woman's?

A rush of blood blemished his cheeks as his gaze fell further down the reflection to a triangle of hair. His jaw dropped. There was no penis; not a vestige; none at all!

He ripped the tape from the full lips.

'I'm Francis, not Frances,' she said with a smile.

His jaw dropped.

'Your aunt was worried that your tastes prevented long term relationships. We hatched a plan. You see? We had a relationship before we had sex. This kind of sex. The sort I like.'

Carew finally found his voice. 'We haven't had sex.'

Her smile broadened. 'Not yet,' she said. 'But we will. We most definitely will.'

Strangers On A Bus
by Nicky B

Cheryl stepped up out of the rain and reached into her bag for her purse; she paid and the humourless bus driver dispensed a ticket.

He blatantly looked her up and down; she was wearing a short skirt and a vest top that was drenched with the rain.

She had no bra on and her nipples protruded through the thin red material.

It was tiring, all these men staring at her all the time.

Why couldn't she wear what she wanted without a big sign above her head stating *Piece of meat*?

As she tore off her ticket, she lifted her sunglasses and looked the driver up and down.

When she looked some more and made eye contact, he blushed and she gave him a 'How does it feel' look, then made her way to the back of the bus.

Damn this British weather!

Cheryl's bare skin itched on the rough seat material so she wiggled around until all the upstanding fibres were flat.

She looked up to the front of the bus to see the driver staring at her in the mirror, she poked her tongue out at him and he went back to keeping his vehicle on the road.

It was starting to get dark outside; all the bus's fluorescent lights were giving out equal but not too bright beams and the décor of the seats and handrails did nothing to improve the interior.

There were half a dozen other people on the bus; most of them were on their way home from boring jobs by the looks on their blank faces.

She found herself looking at a red-headed woman a few seats ahead.

The woman was on a sideways bench so her face was in full view.

Her pale skin and straight bob haircut really caught the attention, her blazing red hair too, and her eyes, both beautiful and treacherous.

She looked around right into Cheryl's eyes; caught off-guard, she quickly looked away.

As she looked away, she could feel the woman staring back at her, feel that her skin was starting to flush.

This rarely happened when a man looked at her, but then – they were always doing it, anyway.

An involuntary reflex made Cheryl look back at the woman and saw that she was not looking at her eyes, but lower. She felt her nipples swelling under her damp top: they were clearly being admired. As the bus moved bumpily along, they rubbed against her top. Her lips parted as she took in a deep breath and her heart began to race.

The woman suddenly made eye contact again; instead of looking away, Cheryl locked gazes with her. A smile graced the woman's pale face; Cheryl felt herself blushing heavily and quickly started rooting through her bag, for nothing in particular.

The bus stopped and a handful of people stood up to leave – including the red haired woman.

While she continued rifling through her bag, she peered out of the corner of her eye to look at the woman.

Why was she leaving?

Her heart sank as she took out her mobile phone to pretend to read text messages, she did not dare look up to see the woman leaving as she knew she would be looking.

Why was her heart sinking? She had never been attracted to a woman before!

As the bus moved off again and she put her phone back into her bag, someone sat right next to her on the seat.

It was the red-haired woman, her grey eyes were looking right into Cheryl's.

She started to speak but the woman quickly put a finger to her lips.

'Shhh!' she said, almost in a whisper and then she turned around to face the front of the bus.

After what seemed like a lifetime, Cheryl felt something on her leg.

It was a hand, a warm hand that was slowly sliding over her bare flesh to her knee.

As she watched it in disbelief, her heart began to pound hard against her rib cage.

The smooth hand moved up and down; down to her knee and each time it returned it moved the tight material of her skirt a little higher.

The palm turned to fingertips, gentle strokes in five places at once all over Cheryl's thigh.

As the fingers slid up to the top, they curled under her skirt material and pulled it up a few inches. Cheryl wanted to stop her, they were on a bus in public, after all, but she just could not bring herself to.

She looked at the red-headed girl; the returned gaze

was a narrowing of eyes to establish who was in charge.

Without thinking Cheryl opened her legs wider, pushing them against the woman, who moved her own out of the way so she could maintain her position. Straight away, fingertips were sliding up and down the edge of her g-string, stroking the very top of her inner thigh. Cheryl tried hard to calm her breathing; a trail of sweat ran down between her breasts as they heaved up and down.

The woman was looking straight ahead now, apparently unaware that her left hand was between a stranger's thighs.

The material was swept aside gently and a soft hand cupped her pussy, it flattened and moved up and down against the wet lips.

Cheryl could not hold back and gave out a loud moan; as she looked around it was clear that it had caught the attention of a couple of the other passengers.

She quickly feigned a sneeze and was no longer centre stage; she looked at the red-head, who had a small smile on the edge of her mouth.

She felt her lips getting wetter as the hand moved up and down, the hand changed to fingertips and, before she could protest, the middle one slid inside her.

The bus rumbled along the wet road and seemed to pick out every pothole, causing the woman to finger fuck Cheryl's pussy.

Knuckles struck the outer of her entrance with each bump; her lip trembled as she bit it – desperate to let the world know how much she loved this, and how much she wanted it.

The short wet finger slid out and was replaced by two, they were curled up inside to press against the upper part of her pussy while the palm pressed against her swollen clit.

The woman had gripped her like a bowling ball and started to move her hand from side to side, the wet walls were stretching inside. Cheryl felt flushed again; her blood was pumping through her veins as if someone was jet washing them from the inside.

The two fingers stirred around inside her, drenched with juices, they slid around easily. The woman moved them faster and Cheryl felt a climax coming close; she gripped the seat tight, using all her strength to control it.

She shook her head so that her sunglasses fell down over her eyes; allowing her to close them tight without detection.

The woman turned to watch her, her face as emotionless as a poker player.

Just when Cheryl thought she was going to tip over the edge, the woman pulled her fingers out. Even through the dark lenses, the woman could tell she was silently begging. Obediently, she returned her still wet fingers and pressed her thumbnail onto Cheryl's swollen clitoris.

She had to hold her breath as a climax tore through her body, like a wild animal trying to claw its way to freedom.

She convulsed on her seat as the woman's fingers milked her climax dry, watching her face intently. Cheryl's breathing slowed in time, along with her heart, sweat running down her chest as she looked again at the woman. She wanted to speak to her, tell her that was the best orgasm for months and the first induced by a women, but she could see there would be no reaction from her.

All she did was lick her fingers clean and place them on her own lap.

Cheryl pulled her g-string across, smoothed her skirt

down and closed her still shaking legs. It would be a while before she could get up to walk, so she was thankful that her stop was not for some time.

This was not the case for the red-headed woman, however, for, just as quickly as she had appeared, she got smartly up and walked to the front of the bus. Giving Cheryl a final look, she smiled very slightly and disembarked into the dark.

Cheryl lifted up her sunglasses and looked through the dirty windows in the hope of catching another glance but she was gone.

She sat back and smiled cheekily to herself – reflecting on what had just happened.

Was it real? A dream?

She gave out a long sigh that was close to a purr and went back to being a silent, discreet passenger again, like everyone else on the bus.

Her stop was just ahead; she rang the bell and walked to the front of the bus. The driver was watching again.

Just as she passed him and alighted, she purposely dropped her bag. She bent right over to pick it up – exposing her smooth buttocks in all their glory. Slowly retrieving her bag, she turned and smiled at the stunned driver and walked off into the night.

While the driver was still in shock, a voice called from behind him.

'Are we going now or what?'

Keeping It Real
by Landon Dixon

'You're with me today, buddy boy,' Connie said, tapping my shoulder.

I scarfed the rest of my doughnut, chugged my coffee, and turned around. Connie Sullivan was one of the 'on-air personalities' at FemNet (the network for females). She was a slick-looking babe, with bouncy brown hair, sparkling brown eyes, and a slim, trim body packaged today in a red satin blouse and ruffled black mini-skirt. She was sadly lacking, however, in the breast department, which for a tit-man like me, was a definite no-no.

'Oh, yeah? Which show?' I asked, gathering up my camera gear.

She flashed a smile. '*Doctor on the House*.'

I groaned. *Doctor on the House* was a reality/medical/Good Samaritan show in which the Network put up the necessary bucks for some broad to get an elective surgery procedure not covered by Canada's Medicare programme. I'd lensed a couple of shows: a woman-whale desperately seeking, and getting, a stomach staple before she exploded; a chinless wonder who received a 'Carol Burnett' courtesy of FemNet's pharmaceutical sponsors.

'Aw, don't look so sad, Jake,' Connie consoled, touching my cheek and pouting her lips. 'This one you're going to like.'

I snorted. 'Blowjob artist in need of knee replacements?'

'You'll see,' she teased. 'Bring the van around front, OK?'

It was an apartment on Alexander. Not Vancouver's nicest neighbourhood, but not its worst, either. Any kind of surgery is big bucks, and if it's not covered by Medicare, it's usually off-limits to most people (except politicians and doctors themselves, of course).

I turned on the camera, its sun-gun, shouldered the equipment and framed Connie in front of the door labelled 401. I gave her the thumbs-up. She wet her lips, pasted a smile on, and then knuckled the door.

It opened, as far as the security chain. A voice squeaked, 'What –'

'Eva Koslo!?' Connie gushed. 'You need a medical procedure that would normally cost you an arm and a leg. Unless … there was a Doctor on the House!'

The door flew open and I almost dropped my camera. Standing in the glaring light were the biggest pair of baby-feeders I'd ever come face-to-floppers with outside of a strip club. They were absolutely huge – triple F-cuppers, minimum; the girl chesting out at a whopping fifty inches, at least. My camera bounced up and down with the gleeful free surgery recipient.

Then the sad reality of the situation hit me like a ton of bricks – this breasty babe probably wanted her lovebags lopped!

Sure enough, Eva was sick and tired of her twenty gallon

jugs, desperately wanted a reduction. And since that was considered elective surgery in British Columbia (a crime against humanity, in my house), she'd e-mailed a plea and picture to the producers of *Doctor on the House*. And now her medical prayers had been answered.

We set up in the living room. I tripoded my camera and got a good, naked-eye view of young Eva. She was cute, with long, straight black hair tied back in a ponytail, a pair of big, expressive blue eyes, a slightly cubby face and body – and a massive set of mammaries! They were tarped by a heavy, black sweater, like she was trying to hide them. The bulky sweater was the first thing I asked her to shed.

'Jake's right, Eva,' Connie agreed. 'Do you have something that shows up your breasts a bit more – for the camera – to highlight your plight?'

Eva retreated to a bedroom, returned wearing a tight, white tank-top, her golden-brown cleavage gaping, her low-hanging, bra-less boobs bulging the thin fabric to the thread and mind-snapping point, her jutting nipples probing for weakness. I inserted my eyeballs back into my head and had the juggsy girl give me a side-shot – a breathtakingly mountainous side-shot that dwarfed even B.C.'s supernatural beauty. Then I had her bend forward, hands on her knees, gigantic tits almost avalanching out of her skimpy top, cleavage yawning open for whatever came its way.

'OK, that's enough,' Connie intervened, as Eva hefted her hooters for the camera, and cameraman, to give some indication of their tremendous poundage.

The two women settled on the couch, did the interview.

Eva whined her rationale for wanting to radically downsize her chest: back pain, neck pain, the pain of

36

shopping for clothes that actually fit, the aggravation of unwanted attention and comments, not being taken seriously by men, jealousy from women, etc, etc ... The list of negatives seemed endless.

But I wasn't shedding any tears over what essentially boiled down to Eva's self-esteem problems; I was weeping at the thought of that bountiful, all-natural babe being mutilated by some plastic surgeon butcher – all that glorious tit-flesh being lost forever!

Connie's cellphone tootled The Bitch is Back. 'I've got to take care of something back at the station,' she informed Eva and me. 'Jake, why don't you get some shots of Eva's bare breasts? That's OK, right, Eva? You knew about that?'

Eva sniffled and nodded, head hanging down. She'd gotten a lot off her chest during the gripe session, but unfortunately, she still wanted more. Unless ... I could do something about it.

Connie departed. Eva sighed and stood up and turned her back to me, reluctantly pulled off her tank-top. She was tanned all over. I had to encourage her, but eventually she turned back around, her arms folded across her mammoth chest, a sullen expression on her pretty face.

I zoomed in on the babe's twin mounds of brown, blue-veined flesh, her whoppers covering most of her stomach, filling all of my lens. I looked up and croaked, 'Can you take your arms away, please?'

She bit her lip and slowly brought her arms down to her sides, her shoulders drooping. I gaped at the hottie's fully-exposed chest like I'd found The Treasure of the Sierra Madre. Her baby-whales swum off her breastbone: immense, sporting inch-long, burnt-sugar nipples and even darker areolas large enough to a set a beer stein on.

37

It was an absolutely jaw-dropping, dick-hardening sight, but the poor girl just didn't seem to realise it.

'They're spectacular!' I wowed.

She glanced up at me, a hopeful flicker in her soulful blue eyes, her face warming crimson.

'You should be truly proud,' I went on. 'Most women would kill to look as beautiful as you do. And most men would kill to look at someone as beautiful as you, like I am.'

She smiled softly, toed the carpet.

'Put your shoulders back,' I instructed. 'Good. Now put your hands on your hips. That's right. And spread your legs further apart.'

Eva did everything I asked, transforming herself from a droopy she-Eyeore into a bold and brazen Mamazon, a jean-clad, bare-chested tit-girl ready to take on all-comers. She knew it, too, and thrust out her chest even more, if that were possible.

'There you go,' I applauded, glancing at my viewfinder. 'Now you just need a little make-up and you'll be perfect.'

'Make-up?'

I quickly brought out a brush, a jar of foundation (on location, you have to be a jack-of-all-trades) and approached Eva, the momentum all in my favour. She looked a little frightened when I poised the brush directly over her overhanging bazooms, but I kept pouring on the praise, building her self-esteem and body-image by reciting all the benefits of having giant boobies; how it went against nature for a breast-blessed woman to disfigure herself.

I feathered the brush over her left nipple, to cut down on the glare, of course, and her jutter sprung up even higher and harder. I caressed her other milk spigot with

38

the silky brush, and her lips trembled.

'Oh, Jake,' she moaned.

I dropped brush and applied hands to the quivering titty-girl, grabbing onto her massive mams. She and I both groaned, she with delight and me with the sheer, sensual weight of her colossal knockers. Her tit-skin was as smooth as a baby's bottom, warm and getting warmer. My damp hands shook as I kneaded that firm, luscious flesh.

I crawled my hands up to her nipples, fingering the rubbery tips of her tits. She gasped and grabbed onto my shoulders. 'Suck my tits, Jake! Suck them!' she implored, as I rolled her rigid nips.

I bent my head down and her left udder up, capturing her achingly-erect nipple in my mouth and hungrily sucking on it.

'God, yes!' she cried.

I swirled my tongue all around her peak, painting her pebbly areola with spit, swallowing her glistening nipple again and pulling on it. I tongued and sucked on her other tit-cap, always gripping and groping her astonishing breasts. I bounced my head back and forth between her heaving casabas, biting into her nipples, tugging on them with my teeth.

'I-I can't take any more!' Eva gasped. Her whole body was shaking, like she was coming. Like most over-endowed women, her mega-tits were super-sensitive to touch and taste.

I forced myself to drop her jumblies. I unbelted and unzipped my pants, as she shimmied out of her jeans and panties. Then I pushed the hard-breathing, flush-faced girl down onto the couch. She lay back and looked up at me, staring at my twitching cock, her outrageous boobs splayed out on either side of her chest.

She pushed her pillows together, breathed, 'Fuck me.'

This wasn't the shy, self-conscious, angst-ridden girl with the overwhelming chest problem any more. This was a wanton, tit-proud sex goddess armoured with humungous breastplates that she knew she could use to lure any man to her honeypot, to her bidding.

I did her bidding, diving onto her overstuffed chest cushions and spearing cock into her pussy. I plunged balls-deep into her tight, wet sex, staring her in the chest and mauling her mounds, mouthing her nipples.

'Yes, fuck me!' she wailed.

I frantically pumped my hips, sawing my raging dong back and forth in her greasy, gripping love tunnel, her boob hills shuddering in my hands and mouth. I torqued it up another notch, pounding cock into her twat, the wet smack of our overheated bodies filling my ears, the tangy-sweet scent of her body spray and pussy filling my nostrils, her galloping melons filling my hands. I fed on her nipples like a starving man.

She shut her eyes and hung onto my neck and whimpered. Then she shivered, jerked, orgasm filling her body like my cock filled her cunt. I fucked her in a frenzy, gripping her mams and dripping with sweat, driving myself over the edge.

'Fuck almighty!' I roared, jisming deep inside her, clinging to her wonder-tits for dear life.

By the time Connie returned, Eva and I were cleaned up and fully-clothed. Connie sniffed the air, sensing that something had happened, confirming it when the interview proceeded and Eva expressed decidedly less hatred towards her overblown breasts.

'OK, that's a wrap,' Connie broke it off after ten minutes. 'Make sure you're at Dr Glieberman's office by eight o'clock tomorrow morning, OK, Eva? We'll film the examination and hopefully get you on the table that afternoon. Won't that be great?'

'Great,' Eva repeated half-heartedly.

'And try to appear as nervous as possible,' Connie advised the 'reality' show participant. 'Make out, even, like you're having second thoughts – it builds the tension.' She turned to me. 'Can you take a cab back to the station, Jake? I need the van.'

Connie disappeared, leaving me behind to pack up my equipment.

I unpacked my equipment.

Eva stripped off her jeans and panties again, then made a slow, seductive show of rolling up her tank-top. Her jumblies shimmied, yearning to flop free, but the saucy girl kept her top half-on, stretched tight across her nipples. The stunning contrast of that mass of hot, brown skin pushing against white, straining fabric made me harder than Mount Capilano.

Eva smiled, rubbing her stomach, moving her small hands up underneath those hanging pumpkins, cupping her obscenely-swollen tits. Her hands overflowed on either side. I panted like a St Bernard, as she finally, slowly pushed her top up higher, freeing her mams in a landslide of flesh.

Her breasts hung loose and xxx-large, and I rushed forward and grabbed onto them. But she wasn't through tit-teasing me just yet. She sank to her knees and gripped my reinvigorated pole, started stroking. I groaned, tilted my head back, then snapped it back down again; I didn't want to miss one second of sighting those naked knockers, especially if their magnificence was going to be history the next day.

Eva stuck out her pink tongue and tickled the tip of

my throbbing dick, swabbing my slit, bouncing my shiny purple helmet up and down on her mischievous tongue. I fumbled the black velvet scrunchie out of her hair and riffled trembling fingers through her silky tresses, as she licked at my shaft.

I shoved my cock up against her plush lips, growled, 'Suck it, baby!'

She stared up at me with her blue pool eyes, her giant tits dangling out of her rolled-up top almost down to the floor. Then she engulfed my cock in her warm, wet mouth. I clutched at her hair and groaned, my eyes bouncing up and down between her over-ripe melons and my lip-locked cock.

'Mmm,' she moaned, sending a thrill racing up my spine, inching her lips down my shaft.

I was soon buried to the hairline in the ultra-busty girl's mouth and throat. And when she snaked out her tongue and licked at my balls, I almost lost it. She steadied me, gathering up her ta-ta's and getting a good, strong sucking rhythm going.

She slid her lips back and forth on my pulsating prick, tongue scouring my shaft. My hands rode her head, eyes feasting on her bounding boobs. 'I wanna tit-fuck you,' I rasped, seconds away from the point of sperm-no-return.

Eva spat me out like I'd said a bad word. She hung her head, becoming the misguided girl again who sees her bountiful boobs as a burden, rather than a blessing.

I took hold of my dripping dick and placed its bloated hood under Eva's chin, cock-levered her head up. 'Remember,' I told her, 'your breasts are something to flaunt, not hide. You want to share them with others who appreciate them for what they are – who think more of you because of them, not less.'

She blinked her eyes and smiled, opened up her tits

and let me slide inside. My cock quivered when it touched smooth, heated chest. My whole body quivered when Eva folded her hot floppers over the top of my cock. I disappeared in that mass of suffocating flesh, and rejoiced.

I bent my knees and started moving my hips, gently tit-fucking the chest-heavy doll. It was slow, satisfying work at first, until Eva spat into her Grand Canyon cleavage, repeatedly, greasing the motion. I slid my cock back and forth in her towering tit-tunnel faster and faster, my swollen cap winking for air at the top of her chest.

'That doesn't feel bad, does it!?' I grunted.

'No – it feels great!' Eva shouted in jubilation. She stuck out her tongue, bumpering my surging cockhead.

I gritted my teeth and brushed Eva's hands away, roughly grabbing onto either side of her bazooms and pumping her cleavage, brutally fucking her melons. She kept her tongue on her cock-rocked chest, on my pistoning cap, her body swaying as I sawed in between her bodacious boobs. I overheated, sweating like a pig, but I kept on churning and churning, giving and getting the tit-fuck of my life.

'I'm coming!' I bellowed. My body jerked and my breast-buried cock exploded, white-hot spunk blasting out of my slit and splashing Eva's tongue and face.

She kept her head down and took it like a woman, lapping up and swallowing my jizz. I was jolted repeatedly, streaking Eva's beaming face with my sticky lust, the awesome pressure of her humungous hooters milking me dry.

Connie and I were at Dr Glieberman's office early the next morning. We set up, then chatted about breast reduction with the not-so-good doctor while we waited for the stars of the show to arrive. Connie subtly enquired about breast enlargement, and Glieberman confirmed that he did that, as well. My opinion of the guy improved.

Finally, at 8:30, Eva made her entrance, looking absolutely spectacular in a form-fitting red dress and red stilettos. Her world-class knockers spilled out the front of the thin garment, her nipples all but piercing the fabric. Glieberman almost had to wire my jaw shut.

'I'm not getting my boobs reduced,' the ravishing titty-dream declared.

'Yes!' I exulted.

'What!?' Connie exclaimed.

Eva smiled at her, winked at me, nodded at Dr Glieberman, a confident, in-control juggsy girl not the least bit afraid of sticking out her chest and facing the world headlights-on. 'In fact, I'm thinking of getting them enlarged.'

The Fitting Room
by Roger Frank Selby

'No way! Goodbye, Colin!' She slammed down the phone in the lingerie department office.

So that was that. Harsh, maybe, but she felt a flood of relief at ending the relationship. What a cheek, saying she was frigid!

Nothing about the relationship had ever felt right. Sure, he was a good-looking lad, but all along, she had been trying to please others – her mother, Colin, his bloody mother ... and when the sex had started, she'd felt nothing – thank God she hadn't let it get too far! And when she said she didn't fancy him, what did he mean by that 'nor fancy any bloke' remark? Was he implying she was a lesbian? Rubbish! That was the standard line from any rejected man. It wasn't that she didn't like sex, it was just that the 'boyfriend' type relationship bored the pants off her. It always had. She wanted something more ... exotic. From now on she would follow her instincts, not try to please others.

She liked her role selling lingerie – it put her on quite a formal relationship with the customer, yet in an intimate setting that she could control. She also quite enjoyed the subject of women's bodies. Measuring them, dressing and undressing them, comparing her own body

45

with those of other women – that didn't make her a lesbian, did it?

The autumnal gloom outside was deep – the clocks had just gone back. It would soon be time to go home.

Then she saw them, a man and a woman examining brassieres in a display. They were a handsome couple, probably in their late thirties. Her fitting would need careful attention to avoid that slightly bumpy line her present garment showed.

'Can I help you?'

'Yes. I'm looking for some underwear that's a little more … interesting.' She smiled and her husband chuckled. They were nice.

Laetitia smiled conspiratorially. 'If you would like to follow me to the fitting room I'll take your measurements and we'll see what's available. Ah, sir … would you like to wait?'

'I'll come along if that's OK, Miss.' A nice surprise. Husbands and male companions usually waited meekly on the seats outside, cowed by the world of brassieres and basques. Instead, he would sit and watch her at work – she bustling around; his eyes level with her … Goodness! She couldn't believe how much she was fantasising!

Inside the cubicle, the stunning young assistant dashed off for a tape measure, leaving the wife to undress.

'What an attractive girl.'

His wife took off her blouse. 'Yes, lovely figure, too. Reminds me of myself a few years ago.'

'That's exactly what I was thinking.'

The girl returned. She had removed her tweed jacket, revealing a simple white blouse beneath.

'Would you like to sit while I take the measurements,

sir?'

Seated, he thought that the sales girl must be aware that his face was only inches from her blouse ... almost touching now, as she reached around his wife. He could see the patterning of her bra through the taut fabric, and a hint of darkness at the tip of a breast.

'Right, madam, I make it between 36 and 38, around a D-cup, depending on the make and style. Very similar to me, actually ... I can show you quite a range. What sort of control are you looking for?'

'Not much; I like my figure to look as natural as possible.'

'You will need at least medium; like me. Anything less and I'm all over the place!' She laughed. 'I won't be a minute.' She dashed off again, closing the curtain behind her.

Sir stood up, imagining her tits all over the place. 'We were right, darling, she even has your figure.' He handled his wife's breasts lightly.

'You flatter me – haven't quite got that uplift any more ... Ohhh, that feels nice,' she sighed softly, 'You don't normally touch me like that when we're out shopping,' she giggled. 'Careful, that girl might come back suddenly – we'll get thrown out! Anyway, I might as well just slip out of this bra, ready to try on the new ones.' She turned away, shrugged out of the shoulder straps and discarded it. His hands reached around and grasped her unfettered breasts. 'Darling,' she whispered. 'You always know how I want to be touched ...'

Laetitia glimpsed the movement as she was about to enter the cubicle. She peeped through the gap. The man was fondling his wife! A wonderful shock went through her lower body. She watched, excited by male hands deeply

47

kneading compliant breasts. The woman's head went back. No man had ever handled Laetitia with such confidence and strong familiarity. When she had allowed it, Colin's touch had been corpse-like.

She coughed before entering, her heart thumping. Sir's hands had vanished from Madam's bare breasts as he sat down, but the finger-marks remained.

'I slipped out of my old bra in preparation. My husband has seen me like this before.' She swung herself around, flaunting herself a little. Madam had pride in her figure. She was in pretty good shape, and with a man who knew what to do. Laetitia felt quite jealous! She desperately wanted to swing herself around like that. Right here. She wondered how Sir would appreciate her younger breasts with their stronger uplift, wondered how it would feel if he handled her in that same, powerful way.

'Of course, madam.' She was a little breathless. 'I've brought a selection you might like to try.'

Madam tried on the three bras. Sir sat and watched. She wondered if he noticed that she was touching Madam's breasts quite frequently as she eased her into place. Madam seemed to like her familiar style.

Two bras were a little on the small side and the other just a fraction too big. Laetitia smiled as she helped Madam out of the third. 'You are exactly the same size as me. We have this same trouble, just between a 36 and a 38 D cup. I have to have mine specially made elsewhere, but it's really worthwhile to get a good fit.' They both gazed at Laetitia's bust as she cupped it with her hands. 'I'll just quickly show you what I mean.' It seemed quite natural for her to take off her blouse and model her special bra. It felt good. She knew her breasts were practically out on view, but the bra made it OK. This was

her job. 'Notice how the top of the cup does not dig in –
it's a snug fit.' She slid a finger between the surface of
her breast and the material, plucking it away a little on
each side. Madam noticed, and so did Sir.

Laetitia had the smoothest, creamiest skin – almost ivory
against the semi-transparent material. Sir saw the dark,
almost conical areola topping each breast. The salesgirl's
nipples – at his eye-level – were clearly visible and quite
erect. 'You can see that each cup follows the natural
line.' She turned from side to side to show each breast in
profile. They swung and bounced slightly, controlled by
the perfect bra. Madam approached, her own unconfined
breasts swinging around a good deal more.
  'Miss ...?'
  'Call me Laetitia, please, madam.'
  'Laetitia. That is just perfect!' Her finger reached out
and brushed the sales girl's skin as she traced the top line
of the left cup where it blended smoothly into the curve
of her breast.
  Sir saw Laetitia react to his wife's gentle touch on the
upper parts of her superb breasts. He saw her eyes close
for a moment, saw her chin rise a little.
  'Is there a possibility ... that I could ...?'
  'Of course you can, madam.' Her hands reached
around her back instinctively to unhook her bra. In front
of Sir's disbelieving gaze Laetitia released it, slipped off
the shoulder straps and passed the garment to his wife to
try on.
  My God, he thought, there they are; her tits are out,
and they are just gorgeous! Although superficially like
his wife's, they had amazing uplift and more prominent,
well-formed nipples. He could hardly stop himself
reaching out for them as they jiggled about in front of his

nose. He felt his heart beating powerfully, his loins stirring.

This 'Laetitia' was clearly a game girl! She must know it's going a little too far, he mused. Just modelling the bra had been pushing it, especially in front of him. Maybe with his wife prancing about with her boobs out, it had seemed natural to join her. He could see how that would be acceptable with the women on their own, but in front of him …. Wow!

His wife held the bra between the two sets of bare breasts for a moment. 'Actually Laetitia, I was only going to ask you where you had it made.'

'Oh!' It was as if she suddenly became aware of herself standing there, her tits out in front of Madam's husband. She half reached out for the bra, covering herself with her elbows as she did. She blushed deeply.

'But as you have so kindly offered, I might just as well try it on for size!' she said, with a big smile that included him.

He pretended to watch his wife as she donned the bra. The sales girl had given up trying to cover herself – a difficult task anyway, for a well-made girl like her, so the hands that had reached out to recover her modesty, now assisted Madam in the fitting. He guessed she was trying to be all business-like to cover her embarrassment. What a lovely woman she was! The blush had spread down her chest and upper arms, but not to the quivering tips of her tits, he noticed.

'Is everything all right Laetitia? Do you need any help in there?'

The authoritative voice from just outside, made them all jump like naughty children.

'Ah, yes, Mrs Giles … We are fine, thank you.'

'OK, then. We'll be closing in five minutes.'

The spell was broken.

'Lingerie department, Laetitia speaking, how may I help?'

'It's Mrs Brown.'

'Oh, hello, Mrs Brown.' Her telephone voice was friendly – very mellow.

'Hello, Laetitia. We left in a bit of a rush last week … I was wondering if you could give me that bra manufacturer's name and phone number?' Laetitia seemed to have the details handy. Madam carefully wrote it down, reading back the number. 'Thank you, Laetitia. I hope you didn't get into any trouble … over last week?'

'No, Mrs Brown, not at all. I'm very sorry if I offended your husband. I went a bit too far … It was a silly thing to do.'

'No, not at all, it was all very natural and … very beautiful. In fact,' she lowered her voice to a conspiratorial tone, 'he's hardly spoken of anything else all weekend!'

Laetitia couldn't help joining in Mrs Brown's chuckle. She'd also been thinking a lot about the experience. How wonderful it had felt, even when she realised she had overdone it. She was so glad the man had enjoyed seeing her body, her breasts … Her breath was coming a little short as she recalled his gaze upon her …

'Look, Laetitia, I don't know quite how to say this, but is there any way …?'

'… we could get together again?' She was amazed at herself for phrasing it that way.

'Why yes! It was fun, wasn't it? I'm glad you saw it the same way we did.'

'Yes, it was … Well, you could always come for another fitting, er … Mrs Brown. Shall I call you that?'

'Call me Madam, as before.'

Laetitia caught on at once. 'Would you like to arrange another fitting then, madam?'

'When would be convenient?'

She paused. 'About three this afternoon, madam.'

'May I bring my husband? I would like him to be shown some different styles ... To see which he likes best.'

'Certainly, madam. I will happily show him all I can offer."

After she had put down the phone, she held on to it for a few moments, until the rise and fall of her breasts became less noticeable.

Monday afternoon was always quiet, and Mrs Giles wouldn't be back till four. When the couple arrived, the exchange of glances was electric.

'Good afternoon, madam, sir. I've found several items that might be of interest.'

She led them to the fitting room more nervously than before. Offering Sir a seat, she couldn't help noticing his embarrassment. He sat down quickly, a strategically placed arm covering the beginnings of his arousal. She had a flickering of alarm at the clear evidence of Sir's considerable male member – maybe she hadn't thought this through ... But Madam wasted no time, took off her frilly blouse, and was immediately naked to the waist. Her slightly heavy breasts moved beautifully. The sight calmed Laetitia. She wanted to hold them.

'If you would like to try this one, madam?' She offered the first bra.

'Actually, Laetitia, I was wondering if you could model it for me?'

'Madam doesn't want to try it on?'

'I will be sitting on my husband's lap.'

'Oh!' Laetitia watched as Madam decorously sat on Sir's lap, lifting her long skirt up at the back. She caught a brief glimpse of her thigh and buttock bare to her hip, before the skirt covered her again. He cupped his wife's exposed breasts. The couple watched her, but Laetitia couldn't take her eyes off the big hands gently fondling Madam's bust. 'Oh.'

'I'm sorry, Laetitia.' Madam began to rise. 'I can see this isn't going to work.'

Laetitia got a grip on herself. 'No, madam,' she said firmly, 'I'll be happy to model it for you both.' Laetitia half turned away and stripped to the waist, aware she was revealing in swinging profile the breasts both Sir and Madam had been talking about.

'How about this one?' She swung her body around in front of them while Sir deeply fondled his wife.

'Ahh, that's beautiful …. Ahh, can you lean a little closer?' Laetitia leant closer and Madam felt the shape of the cups and the fullness within.

'May I?' Sir also felt their shape and texture. 'Lovely,' he said, fondling her left breast very gently. Her heart pounded.

Laetitia pushed herself onto his touch, then swung around so he could feel her other breast.

'I have another bra that Sir might like especially,' she said a little breathlessly.

'Show me, please.'

Modestly, Laetitia turned her slim back to them as she changed bras. She was aware the couple could still see her via the wall mirrors but it seemed the right thing to do. When she had adjusted herself carefully, she turned back again.

'Wow!' Sir was impressed. She was wearing what

women call a 'quarter' cup bra. More like a tenth! Laetitia's semi-nudity was now quite deliberate. Her bare tits, lifted even higher by the bra's support, had that X-rated look. 'Wow,' he said again, not quite knowing where to go from here without sounding crude. Laetitia had certainly moved things forward.

She modelled the scanty garment exactly like the previous, swinging from side to side. This time her uncovered, uncontrolled bosom was more mobile. His body responded as he lightly touched her nipples.

'You feel uncomfortable, darling. Would you like me to lift for a moment while you … adjust yourself?' Madam hovered while he wrestled and discreetly released his straining cock under the cover of her skirt.

'Ah, that's better! Ahhhh …' He guided his wife gently back onto his lap. With the slightest of wiggles and gasps, she went, slowly, all the way down and he went all the way up into her tight wetness, firmly impaling her as he held her hips.

Laetitia had stopped moving. Her mouth dropped open. She looked very young and beautiful to the coupled couple.

Laetitia suddenly knew what she wanted. She moved much closer, pushing her breasts into contact with the other woman's; nipple to nipple. Madam cupped Laetitia's soft flesh, leant forward and gently took each upstanding breast to her lips. Laetitia reached out with both hands and held Madam's breasts at last. Then Sir's touch was upon Laetitia's body. She felt the deep, masculine tit-handling she had seen the first time they'd met.

Madam began sliding up and down in a slow, experienced way.

'Ahh, damn skirt, ahhh …'

Laetitia helpfully lifted Madam's skirt to her waist. She could now see all the action, see Sir's stiff rod pumping up into Madam. My God, compared with Colin, Sir was enormous! 'Is that better, madam?'

'Ahh, yes … Would you like to …? Ahh …'

'Certainly, madam.' Laetitia's fingers touched the couple at their joining, her fingers straying first north, into Madam's more familiar territory, and then south …

Laetitia's hands were around the base of Sir's moving shaft, gently squeezing.

'Ahhh.' He gave her breasts an extra hard squeeze and she gasped. Her fingers cradled and lifted his heavy balls, and then she felt the increased urgency of his motion as he began to explode into his wife, thrusting up, up …

Laetitia felt Sir's semen spurting past the tube of flesh under her fingers, imagining how Madam could feel it filling her up. She felt hot fluids seeping back down, warming her caressing hand ….

'Eeeeek! Good heavens above! My God! What is the meaning of all this?'

Mrs Giles had returned early.

'Mrs Brown?'

'Yes?'

'It's me.'

'I'm sorry, who …?' She looked unseeing onto the snow-covered garden. Could it be? 'Laetitia?'

'Yes!'

Her heart leapt. 'But it's been such a long time! We thought …'

'Well, I was dismissed, of course.'

'Oh, I'm so sorry, Laetitia. We were banished as well – lucky not to have a case brought against us, apparently. We tried to get in touch with you, but the store wouldn't help.'

'No, they were horrible, that's why I couldn't reach you.'

'Oh. You were trying to reach us? That's very sweet. We thought after all that, you wouldn't want to know.'

'Not at all! If there was any guilt, then I was guiltier than you both. No. I wanted to find you. I even tried the phone book, but you know how many Browns there are!' They both giggled.

'We're ex-directory, anyway, Laetitia – very middle-class! So how did you get this number?'

'You were on the database of the company I now work for. A good few Browns there, too; I've been working through the list.'

'How nice! I knew a girl like you would always find work. Which company?'

'According2Taste, the Internet company.'

'Ah, yes. We ordered something from them six months ago.'

'Yes, I know.' Laetitia's voice changed slightly as she slipped into her old role. 'I would like to show you some of our latest products, madam. Have you seen our website recently?'

'No, I haven't, but I have it bookmarked.'

'Then if you would like to choose some garments in the exotic lingerie section I would be happy to bring them around to your address – at a convenient time, madam.'

'Yes, Laetitia, that sounds wonderful! Hmm …Would the weekend be OK for you – say Saturday evening, about eight?'

'That will be perfect, madam; and there's no need to order – just e-mail the item numbers to: *Laetitia@According2Taste.co.uk*. My name is spelt with an 'ae'. You can always contact me there, it's private.'

'Hey, look at this, darling!' she said as her husband came home.

'What is it?' He came into the study.

'I've found you something interesting on the Internet.'

Sir looked, and gave out a low whistle. 'My God, that's her! There she is!' And there she was, happily modelling the type of underwear not available at the store they were barred from. Madam scrolled down the pictures. Laetitia appeared frequently, always modelling the most outrageous items that hid little or nothing of her incredible body. 'Darling, is there any way we could contact her again do you think?'

'You must be kidding! Can you imagine how they would respond to an e-mail saying, "Please put me in touch with the model with the nice bottom wearing item so-and-so?" They must get loads of such junk.'

'Yes, of course.'

'Anyway, I'm going to order a few items. They should be here by the weekend; I can surprise you then.'

'Have you put the heating up? It feels damned hot this evening.'

'Just tweaked it up a bit; it's going to snow again tonight.'

The bell rang. 'Are we expecting anyone? Probably bloody carol singers again!'

'Would you get it, darling? I'm just off to change.'

He opened the door. A young woman wearing a white fur coat stood there in the dark. It took a moment for him to recognise her. 'Laetitia! How wonderful!' A flurry of snow blew past her. 'Hey, come straight into the warm.' She came inside and he shut the door. 'What on earth are

57

you doing here?'

'I've brought some samples for Madam.'

'Oh, right … may I take your coat?'

'Thank you, sir.' She turned as she loosened the coat and put down her bag. He caught the coat as she let it slide from her bare shoulders, and there she was, wearing nothing but her shoes and long black gloves. Now he knew why his wife had turned up the thermostat. She turned to face him. 'If Sir would show me to the Fitting Room.' She seemed a little breathless; her outstanding breasts rose and fell, then jiggled as she dipped to retrieve her bag.

'Oh. My wife must have told you about the dressing room.'

'Yes, sir, the Fitting Room; that is where she should be.'

'It's upstairs … after you.' Following Laetitia's gorgeously bare body up the stairs left nothing to his imagination, her round, smooth bottom rolling around her dark pussy. He was very aroused, but strangely nervous.

'So those are samples for Madam to try on?'

'Yes, sir, and she has also ordered something for you to try on too.'

They entered the fitting room. His wife waited there, naked. He felt the odd one out with all his clothes on, but it didn't last long. Both women helped him undress.

'Oh!' gasped Laetitia as he sprang into view.

'Don't worry, Laetitia dear.' Madam held him lovingly. 'He's nothing to be afraid of.'

His wife took him in her mouth, her hands holding his lower shaft and balls. Laetitia approached, offering her superb tits. He reached out and fondled them as his wife sucked.

Laetitia pressed against him and he took the brown tip

of a creamy breast into his mouth. She sighed deeply.

He sampled her other breast, then came up for air. 'So what did you bring for me to try on?'

His wife pointed his readiness up at the girl. Laetitia turned coyly away and bent forward, presenting her beautiful bottom to him. Then she backed up until the glistening tip of him touched her, and spread her lips.

'Me, sir.'

My Immortal
by Sally Quilford

The man on the train kept looking at me, winking, then gesturing to the corridor, presumably to where the toilets were situated. I gave him a look that was as cold as the frost collecting on the window. I wasn't interested in a quickie and, even if I was, he wasn't my type. Not that I have a type nowadays.

'You need to go away for a while,' my friend, Cathy, told me. 'You haven't stopped since James died. It's all very well to throw yourself into work, Vicky, but you need time to grieve too. Why don't you go up to the cottage over the Christmas holidays?' At the time I thought it was Cathy's way of not inviting me to another strained Christmas dinner, but it started to make sense when other friends half-heartedly invited me to their own celebrations. This year I didn't want to be a drain on peoples' emotions. I'd spend time alone and not have to force a smile when I only felt like crawling into bed and dying slowly.

So that's where I was headed, to our cottage in Derbyshire. James and I used to escape there for long weekends of delicious love-making that began on Friday night, and didn't stop until Monday morning. Well, it stopped, of course. No one could have sex for that long without stopping, but it always felt as if we'd made love all weekend. Even eating pizza or lying together watching rubbish on television was an element of our love-making. Every word we spoke was part of the seduction, the most innocent touch a leisurely precursor to another hour of exploration. We knew every inch of each other, and when he died, we still had so much more to learn.

His memory gradually slipped away from me, so that I couldn't remember his body. I couldn't remember his touch. I couldn't remember his kisses. I couldn't remember how it felt when he was inside me. My body was an empty space where he used to be.

I wanted to forget him. If I could do that, it wouldn't hurt any more. For two years I'd avoided the cottage, unable to face the bittersweet memories. Now it was time to exorcise his ghost.

When I arrived at the cottage, it looked so bleak in the snowy landscape that I almost turned around and went straight home. But I pushed the thought aside and plodded on, remembering that the first time we came here in winter, we fell in love with the cottage all over again, because it looked like something off a Christmas card. Inside was dank and dark. The furniture, which should have been familiar, looked as though it belonged to someone else. I felt awkward sitting on the chair, like an interloper.

Half an hour later, struggling to light the fire with damp wood and frozen fingers, the Aga barely warm, and with night drawing in, I admitted defeat and went to bed, wearing all my clothes for warmth. I must have been dozing when I felt a soft kiss on my cheek. I opened my eyes and for a moment I was sure James stood at the side of the bed. Then he was gone.

'No,' I whispered to myself. 'Don't do this. He's not here. He's gone.' I pulled the covers over my head and slept.

I awoke in the morning with the covers thrown off, and heat filling the bedroom. When I got up and touched the radiator, it was hot. Rushing down to the kitchen, I found the Aga not only hot, but with a kettle of water heating on the hob. The fire was blazing, with more logs in the grate. James used to do that when we stayed. Get up early, light the fire, put the kettle on then return to bed until we were ready for our first drink of the day. I pushed the thought away. Obviously the fire had got going after all. Quite who'd kept it stocked up all night, I didn't want to think about.

I took my drink back to bed, and lay among the covers, stretching my fingers out to what used to be James's side of the bed. Trying and failing to find him in the cool cotton sheets. I must have dozed, because when I opened my eyes a little, I was sure I could see a form in the bed next to me. I reached out my hand and felt skin. I reached further and felt the soft down of chest hair. I kept my eyes half closed, afraid that if I opened them fully the sensation would disappear.

'Close your eyes and feel me,' I heard someone whisper, so I did as I was told. Whether this was real or a dream I didn't want it to end.

The covers above me moved a little and I felt warm fingers stroking my collarbone, moving slowly downwards to my breasts. I lay on my back and savoured the sensation of fingers tweaking nipples so they became hard to his touch. When the fingers were replaced with a probing tongue, sweetly tickling my nipples, I gasped, arching my back for more. The hot mouth on my breast moved lower, over my ribs, down to my navel and then...

My mobile phone rang on the bedside table next to me. I opened my eyes and all the sweetness was gone. It was my mother, asking if I was all right. I didn't want to be angry with her. After all, she'd only disturbed a dream, and she had no way of knowing. Yet, when we'd finished talking, I switched my phone off.

'Come back,' I said to the shadows in the bedroom. 'Come back and finish what you started.' But the moment was gone, even though I lay there for quite some time, willing him to return.

I got out of bed, and made myself some breakfast. I was tempted to go back to bed, in case he returned, but it seemed silly in the cold light of day. I dressed in tight jeans and a chunky sweater, then went out for a brisk walk, bought some food from the village shop, then returned for a lonely lunch, all the time wondering if this was how the rest of my life would play out.

After lunch, I lay on the sofa, watching an old James Stewart film on the television. I dozed again, and awoke to hear the zip on my jeans. He was back, so I closed my eyes again, determined not to lose him this time. Warm hands slipped the jeans down, and I helped by kicking them off completely, leaving me lying there in the sweater and my panties. I could feel breath on my belly and fingers – oh, those fingers – caressing me, sliding into my panties and finding my sex, which was still wet from remembering the morning session. His fingers found my clitoris and gently stimulated me. I wanted more. I wanted him to ram his fingers deep into me, to hurt me if he had to so I could feel what I hadn't felt for so long; and I said so, but he controlled me completely, and I was secretly happy to let him. I felt my panties tear and gentle hands move my thighs apart, then the flick of

63

a tongue where his fingers had been. It was like being caressed by a rose petal, the tip of his tongue so soft, so gentle that I wasn't sure if I really felt it or imagined it. I came with tears welling in my eyes, and then he was gone, leaving me wanting so much more.

I awoke some time later, to find I was lying there wearing only my sweater, with the lower half of my body naked. I hadn't closed the curtains so anyone looking in would have seen me. The idea was quite arousing. I blushed and giggled to myself. Either I was going completely insane or the cottage had a very accommodating ghost.

He came to me again that night, just as I was dozing off to sleep. At first I could just see him out of the corner of my eye, lying in the bed next to me, yet I knew that if I turned to look at him, he would disappear again. Our relationship was to be played out half in shadow.

'Who are you?' I asked.

'A memory,' he replied.

'Then make me remember.' I wanted him to kiss me. I wanted to feel his tongue in my mouth and, as I wished it, it happened. We kissed for the longest time, me hardly daring to open my eyes in case I lost him again. I could feel his body above mine, the weight familiar to me. 'James,' I whispered against his hair, as he kissed my throat. 'James, is it you?'

'Hush now, darling,' he said. I felt him lift my hips and the smooth hard feel of him as he entered me. And yet, I hardly felt him at all, not in any physical sense. I was reminded once again of rose petals, as if they were stroking me inside. He was right. He was a memory, not real, and I wanted real.

'Please, harder,' I begged, but he drifted away from me, back into the shadows, leaving me aching for more.

As he went I heard him say, 'Let me go now.'

He didn't come again that night, or the next day. So on Monday I took the train home.

The train had journeyed half way towards my home when I saw the man looking at me. Not the same brash idiot who'd clumsily jerked his head towards the loos on the way. This one was different. Better looking for a start, in a rugged way that suggested he was some sort of lecturer, or academic of some type. He smiled shyly, yet there was obvious attraction in his eyes when he looked at me. I found myself imagining what it might feel like for him to kiss me, but there was no way I was going to have a quickie in the lavatory and he didn't seem the type. He found an excuse to sit near me and we started talking. I'd been right about him. He was a lecturer in archaeology and his name was Andrew.

Andrew got off at my stop, walking a little ahead of me. I thought that was it. I'd lost my chance by being too coy, but at the ticket barrier he stopped and waited for me. I think he asked me if I'd like a drink and I think I said yes, but that was only a precursor to what we really wanted. An hour or so later we were in a hotel room in the centre of London.

We'd barely got through the door when I grabbed him and kissed him hard, wanting to feel skin on my lips and a real body on my fingertips, which I thrust inside his shirt, to feel his chest and scrape my fingernails over his nipples. 'Touch me,' I said, pressing his hand against my breast.

Pushing me against the wall, he pulled my blouse apart and tore at my bra, cupping my breasts in his hands, while we explored each other's mouths. I revelled in the feeling of real hands on my body, with all their imperfections; the slight roughness on his fingers from

65

the work he did, the sharpness of his nails against my hardened nipples; his slight stubble scratching my chin as he sucked at the pulse on my throat. The smell of him, male sweat, aftershave, the slight taste of something – salt perhaps – on his lips. All making him real to me in a way my ghostly lover hadn't been. I felt his rough cheek on my belly as he slid lower down my body, pulling up my skirt, then his tongue, hot and wet, exploring me while his fingers plunged into me. 'Harder,' I said, pushing myself down onto his fingers. I took a handful of his hair in mine, enjoying the texture, pulling slightly, making him groan.

Somehow we got to the bed, and I fell back against it, offering myself to him. 'Make me feel you,' I said. He put a condom on, then thrust into me and I cried out in triumph, bucking my body against his. 'Harder still,' I begged as the bed rocked beneath us, wanting to feel every sensation, pleasure, pain and the burning ache that comes from knowing an orgasm is imminent. Suddenly he flipped me over, entering me from behind, his hands grasping my buttocks, whilst I bit the duvet, trying to stifle my screams as I came. He came soon after, falling against my back, but staying inside me.

He let me cry in his arms, understanding that what we'd just done wasn't only about sex. He asked nothing of me. Later, I took him in my mouth, to give him the pleasure he'd given to me. It was one more sensation I wanted to savour.

I left him sleeping in the early morning light, knowing I'd never see him again, but grateful to him for helping me to feel again.

My immortal had taught me it was time to move on. Chasing James's ghost around the cottage with my eyes half closed wasn't going to bring me happiness. Maybe it wasn't yet time for me to find someone else, but at last I was able to look to the future with eyes fully open and see the ghost of new love somewhere in the distance.

Ladies' Circle
by Kaycie Wolfe

The first time I was invited to the Ladies' Circle within the exclusive gated-village that was our new home, I was left in no doubt as to the ground to be made up before I could truly regard myself one of them. They were a pleasant enough coven, dripping in designer wear, who spoke proudly of their boob-jobs; they even cooed over my little Ford Ka parked on Mirelda's vast drive: 'What a cute little car, Kate, such fun. How are you finding the new BMW Roadster, Lisa? Livelier than the Merc?' A less determined young woman might have cowered in the face of such footballer-wifery; I, however, just took it all in and, after they'd gone, began to re-assess my situation. Merely buying one of the lesser properties in this most desirable of locations was clearly not enough; I had to find a way in.

There are, of course, the more traditional responses the first time a husband strays: scratch the other woman's eyes out; commence divorce proceedings; pitch up at the doctor in tears and get stuck into the Valium, being amongst the most common. Some wives simply decide that two can play at that game, but I had little interest in playing tit-for-tat with Stephen, still less in getting rid of him. What I needed was to get him back under my control, and find a way to keep him there.

As affairs go, it would appear it hardly had time to establish itself. I realise Stephen isn't the sharpest knife in the block when it comes to carving up a life into safe, self-contained little compartments; a necessary skill, I should have thought, for anyone wishing to conduct a successful extra-marital liaison. Not that I consider myself expert in these matters, you understand; my own sexual appetite having been more or less satisfied by twice-weekly congress with my husband, and, when necessary, I'm more than capable of satisfying myself. Orgasms are easy; it's social status that I lust after. Stephen's domestic appetite requires an orderly regime. Sunday roast observes a strict rota over the course of a month: lamb, chicken, beef, pork, in that order, and his sexual needs follow much the same lines, albeit with less variation: on Friday nights, as long as tiredness or alcohol hasn't got the better of us by bedtime; and without fail each Sunday morning.

Stephen's appetites might require an orderly routine, but he is physically untidy by nature, a trail of pens, reading glasses, socks, car keys or diary revealing his progress around the house. If I didn't know him better, I'd almost think he wanted me to find out. Anyone can have a fling, but it takes attention to detail, and bullishness in the face of censure from one's conscience, to maintain an affair over time, and Stephen has neither. Perhaps those aspects of his character are expressed and contained at work, but it's the messy and rather pathetic little boy in him who comes home to me each evening. Stephen is weak; deep down I knew as much when I married him, but mistook it for sensitivity. Oh, he ticked all the right boxes: good looking (he retains a boyish charm even into his thirties), well-mannered, and respectful to women. This was no swaggering, bragging, male I met at a friend's engagement party; this was a fine example of well-bred, prime stock, and I snapped him up. Nine years later, Stephen has progressed to regional manager at the bank, and what with his new salary and annual bonus, and my salary as a primary school teacher, in another year we could think about starting a family. But for now, we've got ourselves a foothold in the kind of neighbourhood I've always set my heart upon. Eden Court Village, with its neat trimmed lawns, elegant water features, and wide drives sporting an array of Range Rovers, Mercedes, and BMWs. And I'm here to stay.

It was his mobile phone, left on the cistern in the downstairs loo, that alerted me; and of course, with the door safely locked, I looked. Well, what proprietorial, keen-eyed wife wouldn't? And there it was, sitting snug between 'Kane' and 'Keith', the solitary, female name Stephen had never seen fit to mention: 'Karen', and with a ring-tone all of her own. The calls history showed numerous conversations over the previous few weeks, but interestingly, no record of any text messages; presumably deleted. When Stephen was in the shower the next morning, I examined his diary, left in his open briefcase in the study. Such trust, such naivety. A 'K' appeared in several lunchtime slots, the most recent followed by a single line struck through the remainder of the afternoon. Not content to deal with vague suspicions, it was evidence I was after, and it wasn't hard to find. Their next assignation was penned in for the following Wednesday at 1.00 p.m. 'K, The Swan.'

My head teacher could not have been more obliging, taking my class from midday to enable me to get to the emergency dental appointment I'd got at one o'clock; she even thanked me profusely for coming in to work so stoically that morning, despite toothache. Around twelve-thirty, I observed Stephen's car pulling out of the bank's private carpark and followed him along the High Street, several cars behind. Twenty minutes later, he turned off a country lane alongside the canal into the car park of a black and white timbered pub. I pulled up in the lane just the other side of the hedge and wound down the window. Almost at once, I heard two car doors slam. The trickiest part was observing them without being seen myself. I eased the car forward past the hedge just as they were striding across the gravel, hand in hand, engrossed in each other's faces. As they reached the entrance, I noticed Stephen hold the door for her, and he gave her arse a proprietorial pat as she stepped inside. I removed from my handbag a pad and envelope and scribbled a short note, 'Be home by 6.00 p.m., or your marriage is over.' Taking the spare set of car keys, I strolled over to Stephen's car, and placed the envelope on the driver's seat.

Back at home, I reversed into poll position at the very front of our embarrassingly narrow drive, leaving Stephen to park on the road, then went inside to run a bath. As I lay basking in the warm suds, I considered how to play my hand. The landline downstairs was first to ring, then a few moments later, my mobile. I ignored them both. By the time my deliberations were complete I felt no need or desire to check voicemail.

Six o'clock is early for Stephen to be home, but he was there on the dot, looking appropriately sheepish; ashen, in fact, as he approached me at the kitchen table.

'Get me a drink,' I ordered.

'Kate ...'

'Did you hear what I said? Get me a drink!'

'Yes dear, of course; what would you like?'

'That's better. Dry white wine, it's in the fridge. I'll be waiting in the lounge.'

I settled myself on the sofa over by the window, and waited. Stephen soon appeared with a bottle and two glasses, set upon a small round tray.

'Did I tell you to get yourself a drink?' I asked, sternly.

'No,' he answered solemnly, eyes downcast.

'Well then, take it back.'

'Kate … please, I can explain.'

'If I want an explanation I'll ask for it,' I snapped, 'Now do as you've been told!' My role model for this tirade was my high school headmistress, Miss Grimshaw, and I'd got her to a 't'. It did the trick, for Stephen retreated into the kitchen, re-appearing a moment later with the same tray minus one glass. He poured the wine and proffered the tray but I made no move to take the glass.

'Put it on the floor at my feet, and do not dare speak until I give you permission.' Stephen's eyes widened and, for one awful moment, I thought he was going to protest, but I sealed his lips with one of Miss Grimshaw's most penetrating glares. I reached for the glass, took a sip, sat back, and embarked upon the speech I'd spent the afternoon rehearsing, and all my life waiting to deliver.

'Stephen, you will neither explain, nor apologise; you will merely listen to what I have to say. Her name is Karen, she is young, pretty, has long dark hair, a wide smiling mouth, and a firm round arse you cannot take your eyes off. You know the moist desire of her lips and tongue, for you have tasted them.' Again his eyes widened, and again I stayed any protest by narrowing mine. 'You make love to her in your dreams,' I continued, gravely, 'and you kiss and fondle her in your

72

car. You nurture your mutual desire over clandestine lunches, texts and phone calls; I have the dates and times. Your next step was to find a bed. I know all this, and more, Stephen, for I have had you followed. I have all the evidence I need, and your dear, sweet parents will be interested in seeing copies of the private detective's report; I'm sure it will do your father's heart condition the world of good. There is no point in protest, Stephen, you are a man undone.'

Countless couples face this moment in their marriage. The wife confronts the errant husband with damning evidence, he confesses, splutters profound apologies for his stupidity in being 'led astray in a moment of weakness.' My own mother bought the line, complete with hook and sinker. And, of course, less than two years later, after it happened again, there she was at her GP, topping up on the Valium; she was on it till she died. My mother was weak, but I am not. I had no interest in eliciting any apologies, or heart-felt promises to toe the line, given under sufferance. I knew I had one chance, and one chance only, to teach Stephen a lesson he would never forget: he may swim freely, and even make the odd splash, but only within the territorial waters of our marriage, where I remain both harbour master, and mistress of the tides.

'Listen closely to me, Stephen,' I went on. 'I neither desire, nor will accept, any apology or excuse. You are guilty of marital treachery and must be punished. Either you leave this house for good this very hour and never come back, or, you will do exactly as I say, in all things great and small, for a defined period of time. There will be no discussion, and no negotiation. Should you choose to leave now, then first thing tomorrow, I shall commence divorce proceedings and, believe me, there will be no going back. However, should you opt to stay, you will obey me without question, regardless of what I ask of you, for a period of precisely one calendar month. Whenever you are in my presence, you will address me as 'Madame Kate'. Remember Stephen, this has been brought about by nothing other than your arrogant assumption that you were capable of carrying on a sexual relationship behind my back, and your misplaced belief that I was weak and dumb enough to allow you to get away with it. You must be taught a lesson, Stephen, until you see once and for all, that I am no naïve, impressionable wife whose needs and feelings can be disregarded at will, but a woman of substance, a woman to be reckoned with. Oh, and one more thing, you shall not touch me in any way, shape or form unless invited to do so. Obey these conditions to a fault, and after one month, the slate will be wiped clean, and you will be fully restored to your former status. Otherwise, leave now, for good. The choice is yours, you have ten seconds and your time starts now.'

If ever I saw a face etched in pain, this was it. Of course, it would have taken next to nothing for Stephen to break such a spell, merely laugh in my face, or fetch another glass and pour himself a fat slug of my wine; next to nothing perhaps, but a lot more than Stephen had in him. I had gambled correctly, for as the eighth second ticked by in my head, Stephen's chin sank to his chest and his lips trembled.

'Yes … Madame Kate,' he whispered.

'So be it,' I replied, 'Now go and prepare supper; the fridge is full, make me something I'd like.'

Stephen is not a bad cook, in fact there are very few things he is truly bad at; it's just that he is pretty average at everything. The fact is, he'd become bland and boring, whereas what I now saw I needed was a husband I could be proud of; a husband my new friends would be impressed by. I'd often wondered how Stephen had got to where he had in the bank, with so much emphasis on sales figures and performance targets in banking these days. I suppose there must be more to him at work than he ever shows at home. Well, if it takes firm management and clear targets to whip him into line then the next month will ensure that he gets it.

It's hard to adequately describe the sense of power I felt in those first few days of Stephen's sentence, knowing I could just click my fingers, order up any small treat or service, and he would obey, without question. I didn't even have to be polite, or smile sweetly, although I often chose to do so. Sometimes, however, I just snapped my fingers, and barked an order: 'Make me a cappuccino/run me a bath/clean my shoes/draw the curtains.' But after a while, I grew used to ordering him to perform such small services, and began to experiment with other commands, such as telling him to do twenty press-ups, or go back upstairs and change his clothes.

'What should I put on, Madame Kate?' he asked, meekly.

'Something I'd like. Surprise me,' I teased, knowing full well that whatever he chose, I would purposely not be impressed. Having made him get changed twice one Saturday morning, I made him drive me to town, where we toured several menswear departments from which I selected various items more stylish than anything he'd have chosen himself. I made him try them all on and come to the changing room entrance to model the results for my approval. I made the final choice, and, of course, he paid for everything. I took him to M&S, where we scoured the lingerie section. I headed off to try on a couple of bras, whilst I sent him off to fetch the matching briefs, knowing how much this would embarrass him. I emerged from the changing room clutching my new bras to find him waiting for me, two pairs of silk and lace panties in hand. 'Good boy, Stephen,' I beamed, and in that moment I almost thought I detected a gleam in Stephen's eye, indicating that, despite the humiliation, he might not be as averse to his punishment as I'd first thought. However, the gleam soon disappeared when I handed him the bras and delivered his next instruction.

'Now take all these across to the check-out and pay for them, I'll meet you in the car.'

It was when Vicki called around a fortnight into Stephen's sentence that the idea really took shape. Stephen was upstairs in the study, doing paperwork for the bank. Of course, I called him down at once and ordered him to fix us both some drinks. Vicki, who is an expensively clad golf widow to a young up-and-coming tour professional, seemed highly impressed.

'Well, I must say, you've got him well trained,' she whispered, as I sent Stephen back to the kitchen for some nibbles to go with our drinks. 'Good-looking too,' she said with a wink.

'You think so, Vicki? Then when he returns you must tell him.'

'Are you sure?' she asked, a little taken aback.

'Quite sure. The occasional compliment is good for a shy husband, it brings out the best in him.'

Vicki gave me an inquisitive stare.

Stephen appeared with a small bowl of stuffed olives, and the remainder of the bottle of wine.

'Madame Kate, Vicki … your *tapas*; I trust you both like olives, and may I top up your drinks?'

And as Vicki lifted her glass from the tray, and slowly

brushed a moist olive along her bottom lip, she gave Stephen her most seductive stare, but her words were addressed directly to me.

'I must say, Kate, you have the most charming husband, and so *very* attentive.'

I smiled back at her, and gave a tiny tilt of the head, much as royalty does in the face of a compliment from a visiting dignitary. Stephen, poor thing, simply blanched, then looked across at me for how to respond. It was then that I realised how completely all the recent discipline had brought him under my control.

'Vicki's given you a compliment, Stephen, aren't you forgetting something?' I nodded in the direction of my guest, whose eyes were still trained on my husband.

'Thank you, Vicki,' he said, 'it is my pleasure and privilege to serve two such fine, beautiful ladies.' And I swore I heard Vicki purr.

'Stephen, leave us alone now, for Vicki and I have important matters to discuss. But first, you may kiss our hands, my guest first.'

Vicki's eyes widened in astonishment, as Stephen leaned forward, proffered his palm, into which Vicki meekly placed her hand, and I watched his fingers fold around it, pull it slightly towards him, then plant a brief but tender kiss on the back of her hand, before performing the exact same ritual upon me.

'Wow,' enthused Vicki, once Stephen had left the room, 'How on earth did you manage that? I'm almost wet for God's sake, Oh, oh my God,' she put her hand to her mouth, 'I'm sorry, Kate, I shouldn't have said … please forgive me, I didn't mean …'

I decided to put the poor girl out of her misery.

'Of course you meant it, Vicki, please don't apologise, there's really no need. Stephen is mine, in all things and in all ways; I am honoured that you find him desirable. It is a wonderful compliment, and I take it as such.'

'Wow …' Vicki whispered again.

I'd instructed Stephen to be home by five on the Friday afternoon, exactly one month to the day since the commencement of his sentence. I had invited Vicki, and four other women from the Ladies' Circle whom she considered the most broad-minded, and I wanted Stephen to prepare canapés. By six-thirty, he had stowed the platters of food in the fridge, along with several bottles of champagne.

'There you are, Madame Kate,' all ready for you when your guests arrive. I'll go upstairs and make myself scarce.'

'Oh no, Stephen, that won't do at all. You are going to wait on us. Now go upstairs and shower.'

'Yes, Madame Kate.'

'Just one more thing,' I said, as he reached the door, 'I want you shave your pubic hair, above and below, every strand. Your attire is laid out on the bed in the spare room. Listen to me, Stephen … you have done well this past month, I have been impressed with the commitment you have shown in obeying my every command. This evening is your last hurdle. Much will be asked of you; rise to the occasion, and you shall awake in the morning with the slate wiped clean. Your smooth-look genitals shall be maintained on a daily basis, as a permanent reminder of your status: not merely a man restored, but indeed, a new man; a man and husband we can both feel proud of.

I looked up from my *House & Gardens* magazine and smiled, approvingly, as Stephen presented himself before me. The chef's apron was one we'd brought back from Barcelona last year, and never used: a plain calico background and, on the bib and front, a black outline drawing of a Spanish bull with a pair of bright purple *cojones* the size of aubergines.

'But Madame Kate, I can't wear just this!' Stephen whimpered.

I gave him the most penetrative stare over the rim of my reading glasses. There was no need for any further reprimand; Stephen lowered his eyes, and recited his mantra.

'Whatever you say, Madame Kate.'

'That's better. Now let me inspect your handiwork with the razor.'

It was as if the whole room fizzed with champagne bubbles; I'd never known a bunch of women so lost for words. Not that the room was silent, as Stephen went around each seat in turn, topping up each woman's glass. Far from it, only the woman he served at any one moment fell silent as he carefully filled her glass; the other four tittered and giggled with schoolgirl amusement at the sight of my husband, naked from the back, apart from the thin red apron strings that dangled tantalisingly just below his buttocks. I, of course, retained a calm aloofness, as befits the composer present at a gala performance of a new composition.

'Another bottle, Stephen, there's a good boy.' My order was dispatched with the quiet authority of one who knows her subject has been well and truly bent to her will, and as soon as he'd left the room a cascade of gasps and giggles erupted from my guests, and they all focused on me, eyes agog.

'How on earth *did* you manage that, Kate?' pleaded Mirelda.

'Ooh, do tell!' the others cooed.

Vicki, who I thought looked more than a little flushed,

simply gushed, 'Wow, Kate, you're amazing, and what a gorgeous arse your man has. Quite hard to resist, if you don't mind me saying.'

'Then don't resist, Vicki, you have my permission to give it a little fondle when he returns, it's quite all right.'

And as Stephen stood before me replenishing my empty glass, Vicki sidled up behind him and gave his cheeks a soft caress with the palm of her hand. Stephen's gave a start, looked to me wide-eyed for instruction, and I gave a little nod and smile of reassurance. It was only as I ran my hand up the inside of his thigh and cupped the loose ball sack that rested butter-soft and smooth in the palm of my hand, that the front of his apron gave a first small twitch, like a hungry squirrel waking from its winter hibernation.

'Hmm, very nice Stephen,' I said, approvingly, 'but I think you should see if any of my guests need topping up.'

Stephen blushed, and as he turned to commence another tour of duty of my Ladies' Circle, I held out my hand and received Vicki's glass, a gesture that not only affirmed my authority, but freed her to fondle him with both hands as he filled their glasses.

'Hmmm, nice *cojones*,' purred Mirelda, as she stared at the bull on the front of the apron, whilst he replenished her glass. 'And, if I'm not mistaken there's something in there trying to get out!'

At this the others collapsed in giggles, their eyes darting back and forth between Stephen and myself, but it was me they were looking to for guidance.

'Well, perhaps we all have a chance to see,' I said, and gave my most regal smile.

Vicki snuggled so close to Stephen that her crotch now pressed against the cheeks of his arse, and Mirelda reached forward, lifting the apron hem to reveal my husband's hairless ball-purse, nestling below a brilliant hard baton, looking her directly in the eye.

Mirelda gasped, but before she could reach out and examine the goods, I issued another command, in a voice all sweetness itself.

'Stephen, I think you'll find Lisa's glass needs filling!' Mirelda looked at me and gave a mock grimace. Deferring to my authority, Mirelda let go of the apron, but her eyes were now on me, and bore a look of undoubted admiration.

As Stephen poured Lisa's champagne, the apron now resembled a circus tent, and Vicki's arms reached around him, raising the hem once more up to his waist.

At the sight of my husband's richly veined cock just inches from her face, Lisa's eyes widened, and a little groan issued from deep in her throat.

'Ohhhh … these olives, look … just wonderful,' she gushed, and glanced across to me for consent.

'Then try one, Lisa,' I said, 'I think we would all need to know if they're as ripe and fresh as they look.'

Mirelda's face was a picture of envy as Lisa calmly placed her hand under Stephen's erect penis, cradled his now hairless balls in the palm of her hand, and began fondling them gently between her thumb and fingers. The others were no longer giggling but straining to gain a closer look and, like a master conductor, I pressed the Hi-Fi remote. As the soft strains of Ravel's *Bolero* began to fill the room, Vicki reached around Stephen's waist, grasped the shaft of Stephen's phallus and began easing the foreskin to and fro over his dark ruby glans. Her slender wrist moved back and forth with the sweet suppleness of a violinist, as she played him in accord with the music's rising rhythms, and all the while Lisa massaged Stephen's smooth balls.

I stood up, drained my champagne glass, and the other three onlookers began a slow, rhythmic handclap. I walked slowly and purposely towards the living tableau; Stephen's eyes were now closed in pained ecstasy and his pelvis began swaying to its own inner beat.

'Not quite yet, Stephen. Wait for the word,' I called above the din. I observed Vicki's and Lisa's every movement, and praised their technique, before leaning forward and whispering in Stephen's ear, 'Now ... now!'

When Stephen came, he made to lurch forward but Vicki clung to him like a lioness bringing down a buffalo, and his hot cum shot straight into my glass in a half-dozen fierce spurts. Lisa shrieked, Vicki groaned, and the three observers gasped in admiration, while Stephen sank to his knees, and I, like a proud matador, rested the sole of my shoe gently upon his thigh, and raised the glass to my lips to savour the spoils. And as I sipped my husband's nectar, I drank in the appreciative, rapturous applause of my new best friends and ardent admirers.

'Stephen,' I said, addressing him directly, 'you've done exceedingly well. Now run along upstairs, take a shower, and wait in my bed until I bring you your reward.' Stephen's face was still flushed from his orgasm, but his eyes smiled up at me, like a faithful spaniel.

Ten minutes later, as I said good night to Vicki and the others, I felt a deep glow of

satisfaction at my month's work, and was not at all tired, but felt a certain spring in my step as I climbed the stairs, thinking only of the new strap-on dildo and jar of KY jelly waiting under the bed.

Begging For It
by Emily Dubberley

I don't like it when men are arrogant. If they act as if they're better than me, I have to take them down a peg or two. Jake was a classic example. I met him at my evening class. I needed to learn Japanese for work and he was a fellow student. He'd lived in Japan for a few years and was taking the class as a refresher. He used to tease me about my pronunciation. I didn't like that at all. Even worse, he used to eye me up, making it clear he was mentally undressing me. He'd slept with half the women in the class and fancied himself as some sort of stud so was always making crass comments, complimenting my cleavage or legs, expecting me to lap it up. He thought that it was his right to ogle me, not realising that some privileges have to be earned.

Luckily, he was a typical man. When he asked me out and I agreed to go for a meal with him, he thought his luck was in. He didn't realise what I was planning. Yes, I admit it, I *had* been making plans involving his naked form. Even though he was an egotistical guttersnipe, he had a certain physical charm: buff pecs, pert buttocks and a handsome face that I couldn't wait to see contorted in pain as he begged me for release.

Dinner went as I'd expected: he kept topping up my

glass to help 'relax' me, flirting with a little too much emphasis on casual touching, letting his eyes linger that bit too long on my cleavage. When he turned the conversation around to sex, I almost yelled 'Bingo!', so predictable were his moves. Of course, this only made it easier for me to manipulate him. I didn't need to make a single tweak to the machinations I'd configured in my fantasies about him.

As he edged closer to me, lowering his voice so that I had to lean forward to hear him, and asked me what really turned me on, I explained that I only had sex if I really liked someone. Or more specifically, if they did as I pleased.

"I always please my woman," he said, smugly.

"I'm not just any woman," I smiled. "I might surprise you with a few of the things I like."

"I've been around the block a few times, sweetheart," he said. "I don't think there's anything that a pretty little thing like you could do to surprise me."

The trap was set.

"Well, if you're a man of experience, I guess that I should invite you back for coffee."

Again, a smug grin plastered itself across his face. I looked forward to wiping it off.

When we got home, I made him a coffee and left him sitting in the kitchen while I excused myself and went to change into my favourite outfit, grabbing my bag of toys on my way out of the bedroom. There's something about wearing full Domme gear that makes it a lot easier to assert my control. I walked into the kitchen and leaned against the door frame. "Are you sure you can please me?" I asked him.

He was certainly surprised but seeing me in thigh-high boots and a tight basque clearly appealed because he hurriedly said yes.

"You will do everything I tell you?"

Again, he agreed.

"This is your last chance to escape. Are you sure that you want to do everything I tell you? If you agree now, we don't stop until I say so."

Jake gulped but was clearly excited at the prospect.

"I'll do whatever you say."

I ordered him to strip. He pulled off his T-shirt, pushed his jeans down and stood in front of me wearing nothing but a tight pair of Calvins. His cock was straining against them despite – or perhaps because of – the humiliation.

"I told you to strip." I barked. "That means everything off. Are you stupid?"

He got naked, revealing a thick cock at least eight inches long and proudly erect. He tried to cover it, embarrassed at being aroused but I slapped his hand away.

"You've been staring at me for long enough. What's the matter? Can't take it back?"

He remained silent, clearly torn between embarrassment and arousal.

"Touch yourself. Stroke that pathetic little cock."

He started at the word 'little'.

"Yes, that's right, little. Call yourself a real man? Still, it's not like I'm going to waste my time touching it. Stroke your cock if you want to please me. Or aren't you even man enough to please me by doing that?"

I looked him straight in the eye as I spoke.

"And don't look at me while you're doing it. You've already had more than enough eyefuls of me. It's your turn to be watched. See how you like it."

Although Jake's movements were reticent, his ever-hardening cock showed that he liked my harsh treatment. Obviously, I'd have to make him suffer for his enjoyment later. But for the moment, I enjoyed watching his hand slide up and down his stiff shaft, his cock-head leaking pre-cum, his thumb rubbing his sensitive glans. I could feel my pussy moistening at the sight but there was no way I was going to let him know that quite yet.

"Spit on your worthless cock," I ordered him.

Again, he flinched, but did as I asked, his saliva lubricating his throbbing member. His hand movements sped, the extra slipperiness enhancing the sensation.

I could see that he was getting close to coming -- something that most certainly wasn't allowed. His face began to contort with lust so I hurriedly moved to him. He was so lost in the sensations his own hand was providing that he didn't have time to refocus his attention before I'd shackled his wrists together with my police issue handcuffs then looped a length of rope between them and pulled his wrists high above his head, leaving his cock bobbing clumsily as I pulled the rope between his thighs and knotted the rope around his waist to hold his arms awkwardly in place.

"What the fuck ..."

The look of confusion on Jake's face was exquisite.

"You don't think that you get to come before I do, you pathetic boy, do you?"

Jake shook his head, his petulant pout clearly revealing that that was exactly what he'd been thinking.

"If you please me enough, maybe I'll be nice. Now, on your knees."

I put one leg up onto a chair in front of him and he did as he was told.

"The rules are simple. You can lick my clit but nowhere else. If you struggle or try to escape your bonds,

I won't let you come all night. And I'll slide this inside your arse."

I pulled a sizeable butt plug out of my bag of tricks.

"And that's if I feel like being kind. You have no idea how bad I can be if you displease me."

Jake was looking genuinely scared, but his hard on showed that he was still getting off on the humiliation I was putting him through.

"Well, what are you waiting for? Lick my cunt."

Jake did as he was told.

He looked ridiculous kneeling between my legs, arms over his head and neck craning forward as if bobbing for apples, but when his tongue touched my clit, I had to grip on to the kitchen table to keep my balance. The boy certainly had skill. His strokes were slow and soft, almost teasing. He used his mouth as much as his tongue, brushing the soft underside of his lower lip over the very tip of my clit, and sucking me into his mouth as if I had a miniature penis between my legs. I stifled my gasps, not wanting him to know the pleasure that he was giving me, as he ran his tongue up and down my clit then moved down to my hole.

As his tongue darted in and out of my pussy, making my clit yearn for more attention, I decided it was time to show him who was boss once more. I grabbed the back of his head and pulled it into my crotch, using the other hand to cover his eyes. I didn't want him to see my pleasure. He was there purely for me to use, to take and to discard. With this thought looping through my mind, I ground my clit into his face, loving the sounds of his stifled breathing and the look of his cock getting ever harder as he licked my sopping pussy. It was only a matter of seconds before I came hard, biting my lip to stop myself from crying out and giving him the satisfaction of knowing he'd pleased me.

I kept hold of the back of his head until I'd recovered from my orgasm, then pushed him away and stood in front of him, looking calm.

"Call that cunnilingus? You really are pathetic," I sneered.

"I want you." He groaned.

I couldn't believe his cheek.

"Did I give you permission to speak? As you may have heard, I want, doesn't get. However, I am in need of some entertainment so …" I sat down on the chair, "...you can finish off that wank now."

He looked as if he was going to cry, realising he was here only to give pleasure, not get it.

"Come on!" I was getting impatient. "If you want to come, come. If not, leave. I should have guessed you weren't hardcore enough to play properly.

Looking hurt at my taunts, Jake put his hand on his cock and started to pump it, rubbing his thumb over its sensitive end.

"You'll have to be quicker than that. My flatmate will be home soon and I'm not letting you stop until you come, even if he does come in."

It was a lie but I was getting bored and wanted to get rid of him so that I could give myself a few more orgasms. I wasn't going to let him see me abandon myself that much. He hadn't earned the right to see my climax.

He pumped harder and faster, clearly worried but desperate to come.

"Do you like wanking for me like a sad pervert? Do you like knowing that I'm watching you and thinking what a pathetic little wanker you are?"

Clearly he did. Almost as soon as the taunts were out

of my mouth, Jake's knees buckled and his cum spurted copiously all over the kitchen table, narrowly missing me.

"You disgusting boy. That was bad. You don't want my flatmate to know you've been wanking over the kitchen table do you? You'd better lick it off."

I knew that I'd pushed him further than he'd ever been pushed before. Jake looked flushed and ashamed as he knelt to lick the table clean of his own cum. I enjoyed seeing the look on his face and would remember it later when I was alone.

"Show me," I said, and smiled as he obediently opened his mouth to show me his own cum.

"At least you can follow some orders. That's a start. Right, all done then."

Jake looked shocked at my dismissal. I tapped my foot impatiently.

"Well, get your clothes on and hurry off home. I've got plans. If you're good, maybe we can meet after next week's class and I can play with you properly. You do realise that I was very gentle with you tonight, don't you?"

"I can see you again?" Jake's eyes were bright with excitement despite his clear anxiety at the thought of what I might inflict on him next week.

"You've still got a lot to do before you learn your lesson. Now, get out of my sight!"

My eyes followed Jake's tight arse as he left my flat. I smiled to myself, already formulating plans for next week's lesson.

Lorelei's Day Of Play
by Chloe Devlin

Lorelei sighed and placed the last dish in the dishwasher. The bowl clanked as she dropped it a little harder than she needed to. But she was pissed. Charles was off on another business trip for the week. He had left last night without even asking if she minded. Quite honestly, she didn't mind. But she would've liked to have been asked.

She was running late this morning for her 10.30 a.m. meeting with the realtor. She'd hoped that Charles would be with her to discuss their plans for buying a house, but obviously she'd have to do it alone. Ah well, she was getting used to doing things alone.

Like sex, for one thing. She'd masturbated again this morning in the shower with the water massage and her pussy was still tingling from the pounding of the water against her flesh.

This load of dishes was the last morning chore she had to finish and then she would leave to meet the realtor. Already it was 10.10. She'd made the bed, vacuumed, done the dishes, even done a load of laundry before getting dressed. But she'd forgotten about the dishes until the last minute. Now, all she had to do was touch up her make up and then she would head out the door for the 20 minute drive and hope she didn't hit any traffic.

A knock on the door startled her. She closed up the dishwasher and went to answer it. Her neighbours, Martin and Gina, stood there, casually dressed in jeans and T-shirts.

"Hi," she said. "What's up?"

Without answering her, they entered her condo, pushing her inside and shutting the door behind them. Immediately they both began to strip.

"What's going on?" Lorelei asked. "What are you guys doing?"

Standing there in his white bikini brief underwear, his cock straining at the fabric, Martin finally answered her. "We saw Charles leave last night. It's the sixth trip in a month that he's taken. So we figured you must be bored and lonely and decided to keep you company."

"I don't need company right now," she said. "I'm late for a meeting with the realtor. We're going to be looking for a house."

"Why would you need to move?" Gina asked as she stepped out of her jeans. "When you've got such great neighbours?"

"But ...but ..." she spluttered, unable to believe that Gina had just stripped down to a skimpy red push-up bra and matching panties. Her words died away as her friend and neighbour started to strip the clothes off her.

"Hey! I have a meeting," she protested, but not as strongly as before. Seeing her sexy neighbour nearly nude was reminding her that the only sex she'd had in the past month was with her water massage.

"Gina and I are going to make you feel so good you're not going to want to move," Martin said. "We plan to give you so much pleasure that Charles will regret leaving you alone."

A shiver ran down Lorelei's spine in anticipation. She

was so horny. Charles hadn't touched her in over a month and she really needed to be fucked – long and hard. Instead of continuing with a fake protest, she began helping them take her clothes off, until she stood there, stripped down to her maroon bra and panties, garter belt and sheer stockings. To hell with the realtor, she thought. She could always reschedule or find another one.

She posed slightly, thrusting her breasts out, feeling her nipples harden under their appreciative gaze. "Is this OK?"

Martin stepped forward and ran one finger down the side of Lorelei's neck, over her chest and circled the taut bud of her breast. "Beautiful," he murmured. "Simply beautiful. I've been waiting a long time to taste you."

Gina laid a hand on her husband's arm. "Are you OK with this, Lori?" she asked. "We don't want to force you into anything. But we love sharing with other people and thought it would be nice to share with you."

Lorelei reached out with her right hand to grasp Gina's breast and knead the soft flesh, while reaching down with her other hand to stroke Martin's hard cock through his underwear. "I'm more than OK with this," she said. "This has been a fantasy of mine for a long time. And I can't think of anyone better to make it come true."

Still holding on to their genitals, she led the pair into the bedroom and onto the king-size bed that dominated the room. She and Charles had made love in a variety of different ways on that bed, doing everything from oral sex to tying each other spread-eagled for a spanking. But nothing had happened there lately except the buzzing of a vibrator.

The one thing they had never done was invite someone else into their bedroom. Yet here she was with not one, but two, other people, and her husband wasn't even here to enjoy it. Tough luck for him, she thought. If he didn't care enough to stay home and take care of her needs, then she had every right to find someone else or two someone elses who would.

Martin and Gina stretched her out between them. He guided her head towards his crotch, while Gina began to play with her pussy through the damp crotch of her panties. She yanked off his underwear, gasping at the size and color of his stiff dick It had been so long, she'd nearly forgotten how beautiful a hard cock looked, with its mushroom capped top and smooth shaft, growing out of a neatly trimmed pubic bush.

She bent her head forwards, capturing the leaking tip between her lips and sucking it into her mouth. Martin lay back as his hands came up to twine themselves in her hair, helping to guide her into a slow rhythm. She licked and sucked on his rigid shaft, bathing it in her saliva as she tried to engulf the entire length in her throat.

She couldn't quite get the entire thing in her throat, but she established a solid up and down movement, feeling the veins in his cock against her swirling tongue. He groaned as she stuck the tip of her tongue into the little hole at the tip before swallowing him once again.

Then it was her turn to groan around her mouthful of cock as she felt a long thin finger penetrate her pussy. Gina had taken Lorelei's panties off and was spreading her pussy lips, while putting a finger or two into her.

She lifted her mouth off Martin's dick long enough to say, "Lick me, please. I need to come so bad."

Gina swiped her tongue up and down the wet surface of her cunt, stopping to rim her asshole at one end and tickle her clit at the other.

"Yes, like that," Lorelei whimpered. "Just like that.

It's even better than my water massage."

"Is that all the sex you've been getting?" the other woman asked.

"Just that and my vibrator," Lorelei admitted, groaning as Gina sucked on her pussy. "But this is even better. Lick me. Make me come."

"I'm going to do better than that," Gina said. "Have you ever been fisted?"

"N-no," she shook her head. "Isn't it hard?"

"Not if it's done right," Martin said. "And Gina's an expert. She'll make you feel things you've never felt before. I've even let her fist my ass once or twice. It was the most devastating thing I've ever experienced."

"Good or bad?"

"Oh, definitely good. But so intense that we save it for really special occasions. Like this."

Gina tickled her clit again, reminding her that it had been weeks since another human being had touched her like this. The touch also let her know that she was working herself into a sexual frenzy. This whole situation was different and extreme – why not go with the flow?

"OK," she agreed. "I'm game for anything once."

"Oh, I think you'll want to do this more than once," Gina said. "Like Martin said, it's devastating and intense, but always brings people back for more. Now, do you have any lubricant?"

"Not really. I don't normally need any with my vibrator."

"Extra virgin olive oil? Cooking oil? Even Crisco?"

"Oh, I think I have a bottle of olive oil. I'm not sure if it's extra virgin or not, though."

"That's OK," Gina replied as she got up off the bed. "You stay here and I'll go check it out."

Lorelei felt the bed spring up as Gina moved off, but

94

didn't pay too much attention as she returned to sucking on Martin's hard cock. She loved the inherent power in giving a guy a blowjob. Men always thought their virility was centered in their dick, and, if they got a women to suck on it, it meant that the men were in control. Little did they know it was the other way around.

When a woman sucked a guy's cock, she was the one in control. If she was a good cocksucker, she could get anything she wanted from the guy, both sexually and financially. Lorelei had never asked for money favours from guys, but she was so good at sucking that she always got her pussy licked for as long as she wanted, and could fuck in any position she desired.

Her tongue swirled over the top of Martin's dick, catching the underside of the head and flicking it. He jerked away, startled at the burst of sensation. She did it again, knowing that it was sending a shot through his groin. Then she opened wide and slid as much of it into her mouth as she could. That mushroom cap tickled the back of her throat and she gripped the base of his shaft with her lips.

She released him when the bed dipped again, signalling that Gina was back. Resting her head in Martin's lap, she watched as Gina uncapped the bottle.

"Extra extra virgin," Gina crowed. "The very best stuff!"

Pouring the liquid over her hand, she rubbed it against Lorelei's already soaking pussy, making sure to coat every inch, every crack with the oil. She even stuck her finger inside Lori's pussy, rubbing around the edge of the hole. When she was done, Gina poured more oil all over her hand, making sure that her fingers and knuckles were properly coated.

Gina looked up. "Are you ready? Ready to experience

more intense pleasure than you could ever have imagined?"

Lorelei nodded. Charles may have lost interest in her body, but this man and woman were restoring her faith in her sexiness. And she wanted whatever they had to give her. "I'm ready."

Gina lifted one of Lori's legs, bracing it against her shoulder and the side of her neck. Holding tight to the thigh, Gina began to insert her fingers into Lorelei's cunt.

Lorelei took a deep breath as first one, then two, then three fingers opened her pussy. She felt wider than she'd ever been before. And there was still more to come.

She jerked a bit as Gina slid the remaining finger and her thumb into her body, forming a cone of fingers that thrust back and forth. "Aah," she said. "That's a lot."

"Ssh," Martin soothed her by petting her hair. "There's more. And you can take it. You'll feel great."

Slowly, Gina began to inch her fingers farther and farther inside, until the widest part of her fist was poised against Lori's cunt, waiting to penetrate. Lori tensed up for a minute, wondering if this was a good idea. A sharp pinch to her right nipple startled her.

"Relax," Martin commanded. "Relax and let Gina fill your soul."

He pinched harder and harder as Gina slid her entire fist into Lorelei's pussy. She felt the muscles stretch wide to accommodate the fist, then close slightly around the wrist. Martin's hand rubbed her taut nipple, causing her to shiver with the dual sensations.

"That's it," Gina said. "I've got the entire thing inside you."

It really didn't feel that different to a big dildo or cunt plug, she thought. Yes, she was full, but that was something she was used to.

Then, Gina started to gently move her fist back and forth inside Lori's cunt, stimulating all the nerve endings in her pussy. And it was too much to bear. Lorelei burst into an orgasm, stiffening her body, straightening her legs and trapping Gina's fist deep inside her body.

Both Martin and Gina understood what was happening and did everything they could to prolong the ecstasy. Martin rubbed and pinched her nipples, while Gina wiggled her fingers inside her.

As she started to come down from the blast of pleasure, she gasped and panted for breath, unable to believe what had just happened. Finally, she sighed, able to feel her muscles begin to relax again, although Gina still had her fist buried deep in her cunt.

"Oh. My. God," she said. "I never dreamed … it could be like that."

"We're not done," Gina said. "I'm going to keep fisting you while you suck Martin's dick. Then I'm going to keep fisting you while I suck his dick. Then I'm going to keep fisting you while he fucks you in the ass."

"See a pattern here?" Martin asked.

Lorelei swallowed hard. That much sex sounded like heaven. But would she be able to take it?

"I'm not going to take my fist out of your cunt until we're done," Gina told her. "I promised you the most intense sex of your life. So just you wait. There is nothing like getting ass-fucked while having a fist in your pussy. Trust me."

The funny thing was she did trust them. "I do," she said. "I'm yours to do whatever you want."

"Then start sucking," Gina ordered. "Martin wants to shoot a load of come down your throat."

She obeyed the order, turning partially on her side so she could slide her mouth down over Martin's cock. As she began to bob her head up and down, Gina continued that slight in and out motion with her fist. Her other hand tickled Lori's clit, keeping her poised on the edge of another orgasm.

It didn't take long for Martin to explode. He must've been on the edge because after a few strokes, he grabbed her head, holding her still. After a few short jabs, he lifted his hips high off the bed, forcing Lorelei to swallow the entire length of his shaft. The come began spurting out of the tip, sliding down her throat, as he twitched through his climax.

She swallowed as fast as she could, trying to breath through her nose. His come was warm and hot and tasted delicious. Finally, he slumped back onto the bed, withdrawing from her open mouth. She took in a deep breath and licked her lips, still aware of the ever-present fist that continued to wiggle and tickle her insides.

"Nice job," Martin said when he could catch his breath. "You have one hot mouth."

"And you have one hot dick. Your come tastes delicious," she returned the compliment.

"My turn," Gina said, still moving her fist inside Lorelei.

"Aw babe, give me a minute to recover," he said. "I'll be ready for your mouth in a minute."

"Fine. While we're waiting, I want Lorelei to suck my pussy. How about a 69?" Gina didn't even wait for her assent before repositioning herself and swinging a leg over Lori's head.

Lorelei felt Gina's fist shift inside her cunt, then looked up to see the other woman's pussy right above her face. She tentatively reached up and grasped Gina's buttocks and drew her down to meet her open mouth.

She stuck out her tongue to meet the wet flesh as Gina

settled into position above her. She licked once, then tasted her lips. This wasn't that bad. In fact, she kinda liked the taste. She started avidly licking, trying to get more and more moisture from the fleshy pussy lips.

Her tongue flashed out, swirling around the clit, flicking that little knob, then thrusting as far into Gina's pussy as she could.

Above her, Gina started pumping her hips against Lori's face, trying to get as much contact from the tonguing as possible. Lori tried to keep the sensations going and bit down on Gina's clit.

That sent the other woman into a frenzy and she pumped even harder. "Oh, God! I'm coming!" she shouted, spasming all over Lorelei's tongue.

Lorelei continued to nip at the sensitive clit, while quickly licking and sucking all around, until Gina slumped down against her body. Then she took a deep breath and let it out, blowing gently on Gina's throbbing flesh.

Gina started to gently move her fist inside Lorelei again as Lori tenderly sucked on the pussy above her.

"I'm ready, honey," Martin said, standing up beside the bed.

Gina got off Lorelei's face so she could watch Martin fuck his wife's mouth. The rhythm of the fist inside her never wavered from the slow steady movement, even as Martin thrust his cock faster and harder into his wife.

"That's it," Lorelei murmured. "Suck him and get him ready. I want him in my ass. Just like you promised."

After a few more sucks, Gina backed off her husband's dick. "There. He's hard." Without removing her fist from Lorelei's body, she rolled over so she was on her back and manoeuvred Lori onto all fours above her. Then she cupped Lori's buttocks with one hand, spreading her asscheeks.

"Here, hon," she said. "All slick and ready for your hard cock."

Martin moved around until he was standing behind Lori. She felt him carefully line up the head of his cock with her asshole. Then, a feeling of being incredibly stuffed filled her as Martin thrust his cock into her ass.

She let Gina and Martin establish a rhythm with her body in the middle. In and out, they both thrust in an alternating rhythm, sending Lori higher and higher. She knew she was going to come again soon. But she was determined to hold off as long as possible to prolong the ecstasy that her neighbours were creating within her body.

"Unh, unh, unh," she grunted as Martin slammed into her from behind. "Oh! Yes, that's it! Fuck me! Both of you! Fuck me hard!"

Then her breath was practically knocked out of her as the thrusts into both her ass and cunt increased. Fireworks started exploding deep within her body as her orgasm overtook her and she shook from the force of it.

Beneath her, she felt Gina pinch her clit, causing her to tighten her muscles, trapping Martin's cock in her rectum. As she did that, she heard Martin give a shout, then slam one final time into her ass.

Warmth bathed her insides as he poured his sperm into her anus in spurt after spurt. She quivered again as he slumped against her back, his cock still hard within her, but spent from the force of his orgasm.

The spasms finally abated within her cunt, leaving her gasping for breath. She turned onto her side, knocking Martin over also as they collapsed on the bed. She drew in a few huge breaths, waiting for her heart to slow its racing beat.

With Martin's cock still in her ass and Gina's fist still buried deep in her cunt, she gave a sigh. "That was unbelievable!"

"Still want to go meet your realtor?" Gina asked, wiggling her fingers inside Lori's pussy.

"Not a chance," Lorelei assured her. "With you guys for neighbours, why should we move?"

"What do you think Charles will say?" Martin asked, his voice rumbling near her ear.

Lorelei clenched her muscles around the two objects still in her body, drawing a slight groan from Martin and a grunt from Gina. "Oh, I don't think we'll have to worry about him," she said. "After I tell him all about this, I don't think he'll be taking too many more business trips. In fact, I think he'll be a very willing participant."

"I sure hope so," Gina said, chuckling. "I've been looking forward to getting that man's cock inside my pussy."

"He's due to come back Thursday afternoon. Why don't we plan a homecoming for him?" Lorelei suggested.

Martin and Gina agreed, and the three of them spent the rest of the afternoon planning their encounter with Lorelei's husband.

New Boots
by Carmel Lockyer

I had no idea I had a domme side, until Bradley got his new boots. They were cowboy boots, given to him by his sister Maryanne when she came back from Texas, and they did something to me, they really did.

I sat at the family lunch-table: me, Bradley, his mum and dad, Maryanne and her boyfriend Rick, and stared at the boots peeking out of their tissue paper wrapping like a pair of ancient dinosaur babies, ready to strike at any flesh that came close enough to serve as dinner. They were ... evil. Evil in a very sexy way.

Bradley wouldn't wear them, of course. He said they were pimp boots. They were massively too big for me, even with two pairs of thick socks on ... yes, I tried. I tried them with black jeans and an old torn T-shirt which I tore further so that one nipple poked through the gap. I tried them with a bikini. They looked best with my long black winter coat and stockings and suspenders, but however I tried them, they looked great on me and I looked great in the bedroom mirror. There was only one problem – I couldn't walk without them sliding off my feet.

'Brad, love,' I said that night as we were curled up watching TV together. 'You're not going to wear those

Texan boots, are you?'

He grunted.

'So why don't I put them on eBay?'

He nodded, eyes still fixed on the football match.

I swear to God that my only intention was to get some money for the boots, but of course, to find out what I should price them at, I needed to do some research. Page after page of boots scrolled under my dancing fingers on eBay. There were alligator-skin boots, hiking boots, Caterpillar boots, thigh-high black patent leather boots ... there were more boots than I'd ever imagined, and all of them fed my fantasy until I was obsessed with boots.

I found a pair of black cowboy boots in my size, with toes so pointy you could have kicked a rattlesnake's eyes out with them, and a fantastic stitched design of spiky cactus in blue leather up the sides. Boots with attitude and really, not badly priced. I bought them outright.

That night in bed, thinking about the cost, I realised I'd have to butter Bradley up a bit or he'd have a fit when they arrived. So when he put his hand on my breast, I wriggled out from under him and got on top. He loves that. I had the imminent arrival of the boots, not Bradley, on my mind, and it was as if I was earning them by being a dirty girl, so I carried on wriggling, kneeling over him and rubbing his cock up and down my slit without letting him inside, while my other hand worked over my breasts. He stared at me like he'd never seen me before, and when I did finally sit down on him, he came within about three thrusts.

'Uh, sorry,' he said.

I don't know what came over me. 'So you bloody should be,' I replied. 'I didn't put in that much effort for you to waste it.'

He blinked. I jumped off him and lay down, full of

sulkiness, then pulled myself up onto my elbows to continue the lecture. 'You just get up there on your knees and pump that shotgun until it's full of bullets,' I said.

'Huh? Are you all right, Sandy?' But he was already on his knees, and there was a stupid grin on his face as he grabbed his cock and held it out over my belly. His other hand went straight to his balls and he began to pull himself. It was weird to watch, I mean just to watch, not to be doing anything myself, almost as if I was controlling what he did. He got hard very fast, which is one of Brad's good points, and then the tendons in his neck started to swell as his hand moved faster.

'Hold it!' I yelled and he jumped like I'd slapped him, but he didn't stop so I reached round and whacked him on the backside. Then he did stop, but the look in his eye wasn't shock. Well, that's not true, it *was* shock, but there was something else there too. Defiance? Challenge? Cockiness? I thought about my boots and stared straight at him as I swatted him again. He stuck out his tongue and slid his hand forward and back, his foreskin making that slick noise it always makes when he's completely lubed with pre-come. I hit him; he wanked. I hit him again; he wanked again. I lost it completely and sat up on the bed, grabbing his hair and pulling his head down across my thighs. Then I laid into him – hard. He was half-laughing and half-complaining and then all I could hear was the meaty sound of my hand hitting his arse and him … coming. I felt the first jet hit the side of my leg and stopped. What the hell was going on?

I suppose I had two choices. I could have let the whole thing die down, as some kind of weird, never-to-be-repeated experiment, or I could push it. I thought about my boots, already packed and winging their way to me, nestled in tissue paper, waiting for me to slide my feet into them. So I pushed it.

When Bradley straightened up, his face red, his eyes not meeting mine, I pointed to the spunk on the bedspread.

'What do you call that?' I demanded.

He rubbed his stubble, refusing to answer, and began to climb off the bed.

'No way, José,' I said. 'You damn well owe me – and you're going to pay. Get back up there and do what I tell you.'

There was a moment where I thought I'd gone too far, and he would either laugh or tell me that things had got too freaky. He rubbed his face again and then he actually knelt back on the bed and took hold of his cock again. I lay back and watched. 'Faster,' I said. 'Slower,' I said. Whatever I said, he did. He wouldn't look at me, but he did everything I told him to. I waited until his thigh muscles were quivering with the strain and then got up on my hands and knees, presenting him with my arse. 'Fuck me,' I said.

I felt the head of his shaft slip inside me. 'Slowly, you're not going to come until I say you can,' I told him and heard him groan.

I closed my eyes and braced my arms, allowing myself to imagine that I was wearing the new boots and nothing else, the heels digging into Brad's calves as he thrust into me. I lifted my hand and began to tease my clit, feeling how wet I was, and Bradley groaned again as he saw what I was doing. I could imagine the feeling of the boots, tight around my calves and ankles and the smell of leather warming up with the friction of our legs sliding around.

'Slowly,' I said again, although it was more of a moan than a word. I imagined making Bradley clean my new boots, sitting naked on the kitchen floor with the polish and brushes, his nice red cock bobbing around as he rubbed my boots with a cloth. I could visualise taking the polish brush out of his hands, and whacking his sweet arse with it, until he was as pink-cheeked as a cherub. I saw myself standing over him as he brought the boots to a mirror shine, and that brought *me* to an explosive climax. I could hear Brad gasping behind me as my cunt muscles grabbed him and held on, but I couldn't find the breath to tell him to hold on.

I didn't need to. Somehow he managed not to come and when my breathing had started to return to normal, I heard a small voice from behind me. 'Sandy? Can I come now?'

What made me say no, I'll never understand, but no was what I said. Then I slid off him and turned around so I was on my back, and spread my legs wide. 'Make me come again,' I said. He pushed into me, watching my face now for any sign that I was close to coming, and fucked me exactly the way I like it, slow and deep, without me having to give him any hints or suggestions, until I came again.

'Now,' I said. 'Now you can come.'

And he said, 'I'd rather ...'

'Yeah?'

'I can wait. I mean ... I ...'

What he meant was, he wanted to suffer. And I wanted him to suffer. So I grabbed all the pillows on the bed and piled them up to make a big heap behind my head; now I could reach round and spank him as he thrust inside me, each thrust coinciding exactly with a slap from me – gentle taps when he was performing as I wanted, harder ones to make him speed up or push himself deeper inside me. Now he was willing to look at me, and I gazed into his innocent blue eyes, so wholesome and boy-next-door that I'd never imagined this kinky side to my other half, as I whacked him like a naughty child. Although he didn't speak, I could tell that the punishment meant as much to him as the penetration, and that he loved the new me who was so willing to make his life a hell, so I made him wait, and wait, and wait, until I was starting to feel raw and he was begging me to let him shoot his load. Which I did, eventually, and after I had, he thanked me. Yes, very politely but also emotionally, as though I'd just got him tickets for the Cup Final. Obviously I'd just given Brad the night of his life.

I lay awake for a long time, thinking about it. Was I ready for this? Could it even happen again or had it been some kind of weird one-off lust-fest which we would never manage to repeat? After a while I realised that I was kidding myself. I was more than ready to do it again, and Brad's reaction showed that he'd follow wherever I led him – the choice was simple, we could go back to boring humping, or I could release my inner dominatrix and show Bradley just how much fun life could be if he let his woman wear the trousers – or the boots.

Speaking of boots, the parcel arrived three days later and the boots were as shiny and pointy as I'd dreamed. I put them in the middle of the bed, on a red cushion as if they were the Crown Jewels, for Brad to see when he got home from work. Then I sat down in the living room, wearing nothing but a smile. In my hand I had a wooden spoon, from the kitchen.

Brad came into the flat and, thinking I wasn't home, went to the bedroom to get changed. He must have seen the boots because there was a long silence before I heard his clothes hitting the floor. Then he came into the living room, naked.

'Bring me my boots,' I said and he turned round and went back out, but I'd seen the hard-on that was sticking out in front of him like a mast.

He came back in with my boots and knelt in front of me. I lifted one foot, I lifted the other – he slid the black leather over my toes and heels and up my legs and I stood. I smacked my hand lightly with the spoon and gestured to the bedroom and he crawled behind me on his hands and knees as I led him to the bed.

'Sandy?' he said, a bit nervously.

I slapped my hand with the spoon again and waited.

'Uh, I think I know where I can get a hat,' he said. 'To go with your boots.'

I grinned and gestured to the bed. I'd already ordered a hat from eBay.

On The Carpet
by Cathy King

My job at Stevens Marchbank, Carpet and Rug Wholesalers, didn't last long. Less than two-and-a-half days, to be exact. And it was all Fran's fault.

Actually, that's not strictly true. It being all Fran's fault, I mean. I should have had more self-control ...

When Beverley Stevens, the sales and distribution director, took me into the Sales Office on my first day, they were all I saw. Eons passed before I managed to drag my eyes upwards to a silky blonde bob out of which shone a pretty face and a friendly smile. By contrast, Beverley Stevens was as flat as a board, and her slash of a mouth looked like it never smiled.

And it certainly wasn't smiling when she introduced me to Fran. It puckered up as if she'd been force-fed a lemon, slice by sour slice.

"This," she said, eyeing Fran's impressive anatomy with disapproval, "is Frances Bell. She'll show you the ropes. Frances, this is Neve McPherson, your new colleague. Please make her welcome." She turned on a low, sensible heel and strode from the office.

Fran got up and leaned across the desk to shake my hand, her spectacular breasts precarious in a low-cut top.

"Nice to meet you, Neve. The company's fairly new, so it's just us till orders increase. I work hard and expect the same from others, but I like a bit of fun too. Unlike Sourpuss."

"Sourpuss …?"

"Bev Stevens, miserable cow. Always moaning about the way I dress. Sent me home once to change into something 'more suitable' but James protested. Said I brightened up the office." She glanced away with a secretive smile.

"Who's James?" I asked, intrigued by that smile.

"James Stevens. The MD and Sourpuss's brother. You'd never guess they were related, though. You'll meet him later, so you'll see what I mean." She glanced up at the clock. "Time to get to work. Drag your chair round, and you can watch what I do for an hour or so before I let you loose on the buyers."

James Stevens popped in to say hello shortly afterwards. He seemed like the sort of bloke you could have a laugh with. Nice-looking, too.

The rest of the morning whizzed by. At one o'clock, Fran set the answerphone and we went for lunch at a nearby pub, where I quickly learned she was twenty-eight and twice divorced. "My fault," she admitted. "I'm just not into monogamy." Ten minutes later, I learned she was bisexual.

And, by five-thirty, I'd discovered I must be too. At least, as far as Fran was concerned. I was tearing off my clothes almost before I'd closed my front door. Then it was into the bedroom and out with Brad, my favourite vibrator. I came in ten seconds flat. And twice more after that. If I hadn't asked an old college friend to supper, I'd have stayed with Brad all night.

*　　　*　　　*

110

Sourpuss was out next day, drumming up new business. Just after morning tea-break, Fran's internal phone rang.

"That was James," she said, putting it down and smoothing her top over the small amount of bosom it covered. "He and Ben have new samples to familiarise me with. Will you be all right on your own for half an hour?"

"Of course," I said, nervous at the prospect, but keen to impress. "Who's Ben, by the way?"

"Ben Marchbank, the other partner. Bit of a hunk, actually." She flashed me a bright-eyed smile, grabbed her bag and hurried from the office.

I managed perfectly well for about fifteen minutes. Then a buyer from a major department store said he always dealt with 'the lovely Frances'. "I don't have time to wait for her to call me back," he loftily replied to my suggestion. "I really must insist that I speak with her right now."

I'd have to do as he asked. I'd be out on my ear if I lost Stevens Marchbank one of their biggest customers. "Hold on, sir, I'll try and locate her for you."

I found the list of extensions and punched in James Stevens's number. "Sorry," I said, "the number's engaged. Are you sure she can't call you back?"

"Completely sure," snapped the arrogant tosser. "Didn't you hear me?"

I tried again. Still engaged. I took a breath and reasoned that if James Stevens was on the phone, he could probably spare Fran for a moment or two. "Sir, may I put you on hold while I go and look for her?"

"You have two minutes, then our business goes elsewhere."

I put Arrogant Tosser on hold, and dashed to the MD's office. A sign hung on the door – *Meeting in*

Progress. Do Not Disturb. I pushed the door open a few inches anyway, and peered inside.

I couldn't believe it. Fran was certainly studying a carpet sample – the office carpet, from her position on all fours. Her skirt was around her waist, and her bare breasts slap-slapped together as a half-naked James Stevens fucked her hard from behind. Fran's hungry mouth gobbled an impressive erection. If it belonged to Ben Marchbank, Fran was right – he was definitely a hunk.

I quickly and quietly closed the door, and staggered back down the corridor on shaky legs, trying to push the erotic image out of my mind so I could concentrate on creating a viable excuse.

By the time I snatched up the phone, I was still blank. "Sorry to have kept you, sir. I'm afraid Frances can't come to phone because ..." I cast around frantically for inspiration. "Because she's no longer here." Totally feeble, but in a way I suppose it was true. After all, she was on her way to heaven, the lucky cow.

"Good God! Had she been ill? I had no idea. Do give her family my sincere condolences."

I hid a snort of laughter behind my hand, relieved at my freak success.

"Well," he continued, sounding quite human now, "I suppose I'll have to give the order to you, my dear."

Yes, I thought, still shaking with suppressed laughter, I suppose you will.

Fran reappeared and gave me the gen on a new range of twist piles, so it hadn't been a complete lie after all.

Needless to say, I spent the evening with my best mate Brad, succumbing to exhaustion at midnight, when the last battery ran out.

*   *   *

112

A secret rug audit had been arranged for the following day. Sourpuss was convinced the warehouse manager and his two warehouse operatives were making off with stock, and had sent them on a one-day course to get them out of the way without arousing their suspicions. Fran and I were to do the stock counts during the morning, check them against computer records, and then Sourpuss would come in during the afternoon to assess the results.

It was the first time I'd been down to the warehouse. Fran led me through a bewildering array of carpet rolls in every imaginable colour, and all shades in between, to an area where the rugs were stored. They were heaped on pallets and arranged in type, size, colour and pattern. It looked like we had our work cut out.

By ten o'clock I was already beginning to flag. It was hot and airless in the warehouse, something Fran was clearly aware of. She'd come to work dressed in a tiny cotton sundress, which left little to the imagination, while I was in my usual uniform of smart black trousers and acrylic sweater.

I'd been wondering for a while why she seemed so uptight that day. I put my hand on her arm, and she pulled the clipboard protectively towards her. I frowned. "Are you OK? You seem a little ... distracted."

"Of course I'm OK," she snapped. "Why wouldn't I be?" Then her face softened. "Sorry, Neve. It must be the heat. Let's have a break."

She sat down on the pile of sheepskin rugs we'd just finished counting. "Gosh, it's hot in here." She looked up at me, her fringe dark with perspiration. "You must be boiling in that outfit."

"I am," I said, wiping sweat from my forehead with the back of my hand as I sank down beside her. "My sweater's sticking to me."

"Take it off, then," she said matter-of-factly. "There's only you and me here. Sourpuss won't be in till this afternoon, and James and Ben are out today."

I laughed. "Don't be daft! I can't just strip off!" Though the thought of Fran seeing me in nothing but my underwear was rather appealing. My pussy (permanently swollen since Monday morning, thanks to Fran) gave a little throb of excitement, then another.

"Of course you can." She grasped the hem of my sweater. "Come on, lift your arms."

To my amazement, I found my arms obediently following instructions, and seconds later my sweater was off.

"Wow, Neve! Why on earth have you been keeping those under wraps? They're fabulous."

I felt myself blushing to the roots of my hair. I'd always been quite proud of my breasts, but I no longer thought they were much to get excited about, not compared to Fran's.

"Thanks," I said shyly, suddenly finding the warehouse floor of enormous interest.

"Stand up," she ordered. "Let's get those trousers off too."

Again, I found myself doing her bidding. She unhooked the waistband and unzipped me while I stared into her cleavage, wishing I could bury my face there and lick her all over, like I'd done in my night-time fantasies. I stepped out of my trousers, and realised my panties were soaked. Could Fran hear my heart galloping away inside my chest ...? Whether she did or not, she realised immediately how turned on I was.

"Oh, Neve," she murmured. She ran a gentle finger over my swollen clitoris, encased in its satin prison. I sucked in a sharp breath and a shiver ran through my entire body. Despite the heat, my nipples hardened and poked through the flimsy fabric of my bra.

Stretching her arms above her head, Fran flopped back on the rug pile, her eyes sliding over my body, her short dress sliding up her thighs. I was surprised – but not displeased – to see she wasn't wearing knickers. Her pink, juicy labia peeped out from beneath a sliver of pubic hair.

Trembling, and wondering if I was dreaming, I reached back and undid my bra, letting it fall to the floor. The wet panties went the same way. Fran got to her feet, quickly unbuttoning her dress, and that too slipped to the floor. There she was, the object of my desire, completely naked before me. I could hardly believe it. My shaking hands reached for her gorgeous breasts, stroking every inch. Her nipples grew bigger and harder. I gently lifted her left breast to my salivating mouth. Then I did the same with the right. Alternating between them, I greedily licked and sucked. Hot juices trickled down my thighs from my wildly throbbing cunt.

"Lie down with me," gasped Fran. "Let's finger fuck."

We toppled onto the sheepskin rugs side by side and turned to face one another. Our bodies fused in a mass of heaving flesh as our mouths met. Fran's right hand slid over my hip and down to my mound. Fingers slid into my dripping hole, and an expert thumb fastened on my slippery clit and went to work. A novice, I mirrored the actions of her right hand with my left. Her clit was bigger than mine, about half-an-inch long, and drowning in her juices. I didn't want to come too quickly, but I couldn't stop myself. Filled with Fran's thrusting fingers, my clit pushing hard against her circling thumb, my orgasm shuddered through me. Then she was coming too, her juices washing over my hand.

Slick with sweat and other bodily fluids, we lay together for a minute, slowly coming down from our sexual high.

Fran was the first to speak. "Wow! That was fantastic. But do you know what I fancy now? A big, juicy cock."

I giggled. "Funny you should say that. So do I!"

"Well girls," said a male voice, very close, "your wish is our command."

I gasped at the unexpectedness of it and so did Fran, so I knew she hadn't planned it.

They must have been watching for a while – they were both completely naked and fully erect. I wondered again if I was dreaming.

Fran laughed. "There's no hope for you guys. I might have known you'd turn up. I hope you're prepared?"

"Of course," said Ben. He ripped open a foil package with his teeth and extracted a condom.

Fran rolled over on all fours and thrust her buttocks up in fuck-me-now invitation. This was obviously her favourite position. Ben climbed on the rugs. As he knee-walked towards Fran's rear, I couldn't take my eyes off his cock. Curving up towards the roof, it was huge and veiny, and bounced as he moved into position, as if it was on a spring. Placing the condom on the fat, shiny head, he rolled it on. Then, resting a hand on Fran's lower back, he slid his cock oh so slowly inside her.

Fran let out a long groan. "Oh yes," she breathed. "Oh *yes*."

Suddenly nervous, I looked at James. This was the MD, for God's sake. I shouldn't be doing this … but I ached for cock. I shyly parted my legs, and James got on the pallet with us and knelt between my thighs. He grasped his condomed cock and rubbed it all over my clit and labia till I couldn't stand it any more. He probed at the entrance to my pulsing hole, then pushed his dick in gradually, inch by rigid inch. Then all of it was inside me and any remaining shyness vanished. Wrapping my legs around him, I felt like I was filled with cock all the way up to my ribcage.

James copied Ben's slow, purposeful rhythm. Fran and I looked at one another, and I knew that my expression must be identical to hers – one of total ecstasy. Eyes locked, we abandoned ourselves to the exquisite feel and sound of hot, hard cocks pistoning our slurping cunts at an ever-increasing rate. From where I lay, I could see Ben's enormous dick each time it emerged from Fran, coated with fuck juice. Faster and faster James and Ben went, in perfect unison. And in perfect unison, Fran and I came, our shrieks of delight echoing up to the warehouse roof.

James grew even larger inside my bucking body, and I knew he was about to shoot his load. That's when I saw her, over the bunched muscles of James's shoulder...

After that, there was no reason for them not to own up to Beverley 'Sourpuss' Stevens. Fran, James and Ben had ruined a few rugs when 'working late' and had been forced to dump them. I realised later that Fran had been protective of her clipboard because she'd altered the relevant counts so that innocent warehouse staff wouldn't lose their jobs. No wonder she'd been so uptight.

Not surprisingly, Fran and I were fired. Sourpuss told James and Ben she'd leave if they objected, and take her money and expertise with her, so that was that.

But the four of us meet once a week, and Fran and I intend to buy a place together – once we find work, that is! So it might have been the shortest job ever, but it was also the absolute best.

Pants On Fire
by Sommer Marsden

It's the first warm day of the year. Something about that first really warm day always makes me feel sexy. Ready to shed clothes and show some skin. Even if that skin is pale from months of sweaters and jeans. But I like to bask in the sun on the first warm day. Marc likes to grill.

The skirt is new. The panties are small. Flip-flops on my feet and painted toenails. A short-sleeved deep v-neck tee and I'm in heaven. I want to feel the wind on my face and my skin. Smell the fresh-cut grass. The neighborhood is alive with the sounds of lawnmowers and week whackers. I listen to my thongs as I walk and I can't help but laugh.

Thwack, thwack...thwack twhack...

The sounds of spring.

"Chicken. I'm thinking chicken with barbeque sauce. Green beans. You can steam those inside and maybe some fresh bread." His handsome face is hopeful and alive and glowing from being kissed by the sun. It seems like we haven't seen the sun in months.

"Why is it that your head always turns to food when the weather turns?" I laugh.

"Michelle, need to know that man make fire. Man make fire then man make food," he grunts at me and

118

when I pass him, he smacks my ass hard and I let out a little yelp.

"Hands to yourself," I snort and lower myself onto the chaise longue. I stretch my long legs out and sigh with happiness. I'll let them get just a touch of sun and then I'll coat myself in SPF 45 from head to toe.

"Why? You're gonna prance around in that … what is that? Is that scrap of denim supposed to be a skirt?"

I laugh again and close my eyes. In a moment he'll be back to food and fire.

"And a deep v. See how deep that v is. It makes me want to stick my face between your tits."

I'm smiling, eyes still closed, but his banter is making me wet. Between my legs a nice steady moist pulse has begun. "Hmmm," I say, noncommittally.

"You've painted your toenails. Let's see. What should we call that colour."

'Sweet Wine'

"Vixen red. That's it. That colour is most certainly meant to seduce men with spring fever. And then the flip-flops. Well, might I say, nothing like long toes and elegant feet."

I almost laugh again but it dies in my throat because now he is caressing my foot and the feeling of his hand on me shoots straight to my center. Someone touching my feet has never been a big turn on but now, all of a sudden, it is staggering in its sensuality. His hand circles my ankle, gripping me, and just stays there. My skin feels like it's circled with fire where his skin is touching my skin. The sun that was just warm a few moments before is now a searing heat and I feel my skin flush but I shiver.

"And then we have your legs," he goes on.

"The same legs I've always had," I attempt to tease,

119

but my voice is taut and my cunt is thumping and my nipples have pebbled against my blouse. What I really want to do is moan, not tease.

"The same legs I have been obsessed with all these years," he teases back but his voice is much more in control than mine. He releases my ankle and his hands are sliding up the insides of my thighs. I twitch under the pressure. He reaches the hem of my short skirt and stops, fingers splayed up under the fabric. So close to my panties. So close to the part of me that wants him the most. He stops. Right there. And lets his hands rest innocently on my skin. My mouth is dry and my pulse is pounding in my ears.

"You're stopping?" I whisper.

"All I'm interested in is food, remember?" His deep throaty laugh fills my ears. I keep my eyes closed because if I see that evil smile I just might die of frustration.

"True. Mostly."

"Am I interested in food. Or am I interested in eating?"

That gets me. Right there. My breath freezes in my throat. "We'd have to go inside."

"Now why would we go inside on a lovely day like this."

A little pool of my own hot moisture escapes me and my panties are sticking to my clit. I would do anything to have them off me at that moment. To let the warm spring breeze blow over my naked sex.

He reads my mind, pushes his fingers up higher and strokes the drenched cotton crotch of my panties. I hear myself make a low sound. A sex sound. He lets me plead with my noises for a minute and then hooks the sides of my panties with his fingers and tugs them off. We're outside in the sun on a lounger and he's going to fuck me. Of that I am certain. The fact that we could be seen somehow makes it better. High fence or not, you just never know who's looking out of their upstairs window on a beautiful spring day.

I have my eyes clamped shut and I'm doing my best to breathe. He slides a finger into me, plays me softly at first. Even though I can't see him, I can somehow feel his head moving toward me. I can feel the air shift and change around me. And then his mouth is clamped onto me, wet and burning and I push up. Grind up. Force myself against his lips and tongue in demanding, steady bucks of my hips.

Warm and slick and quick his mouth moves over me. Never giving me time to adjust or sink into the pleasure. Constantly shifting his rhythm and pressure. Another finger joins the first and then a third. I feel myself stretch and pulse because the fullness is intoxicating. He withdraws the third finger and slides it slowly into my ass. Hand trapped inside of me, mouth smashed against me.

I sigh. When I come it's long and liquid and makes me feel boneless. Marc doesn't stop, though, that is his favorite thing. To just keep going, getting every drop of me he can. He knows me so well that his licks and kisses are feather-light now. I am sensitive and each drag of his tongue is an exquisite torment.

He flexes his fingers deep inside of me, coaxing every last flitter and spasm from my cunt and his voice is raspy when he says, "Turn over on your belly."

I turn without question. The sun that has been staining the inside of my eyelids red is now warming the back of my long, dark hair. I lay on my belly and he pulls his fingers free of me. I feel empty for a moment. The sound of his zipper tells me it won't be for long.

When he climbs on the chaise it groans with the added weight but holds. His cock nudges me, pushing insistently. He slides into me with a groan and I press my legs together hard to make my entrance even tighter.

"Fuck." That's all he says.

I nod. Yes, please. Fuck.

His body is pressed against mine, covering me and shielding me from the sun. I love the feel of him, slow and easy but with a barely restrained urgency. For just a second I remember that someone could be watching us right now. Watching as he fucks me from behind surrounded by bright green grass, glaring sun and butterflies. I tighten again and a shiver works along my spine.

"Will you come for me again?" he says and I can only nod.

For just a second his cock slips free of me. I take the time to slide my hands under my hip bones to angle myself higher. I let my fingers play over my swollen clit as he tries to enter me again. For just a second the head of his cock presses against my ass and he groans. That's what he would like. I know this and I smile.

Then he's back in me, sliding in and nearly out. Dragging out each second of friction and pressure. I stroke my clit harder until with a final forceful thrust I come again. A painted rainbow streaking behind my eyelids. I press my face into the mesh lawn chair to stifle my cries.

Marc continues to fuck me, slow and easy now. I can't help myself. I turn my head and with a voice weak from orgasm I say, "You really want to fuck me up the ass, don't you?"

"That's not why I'm doing this," he says, steadying

himself on two strong arms. Staying still inside of me. The length of his cock steady and hard inside me.

"Liar."

"Not lying." I can hear the smile in his voice.

"Liar, liar pants on fire," I taunt.

"Pants on fire," he concedes with a chuckle.

"Go on then," I say and lift my hips, forcing him to move with me.

"Ah, Michelle…" he says and it sounds almost like he's praying.

When he slicks me with my own juices I relax into it. Gone is my fear of this act. It took me some time to like it. Now I crave it at times. Times like now. He slides one finger into my ass, slowly and carefully stretching me until my body gives in and relaxes. Then a second finger. He flexes inside of me and my heartbeat speeds up my pussy thump. Newly empty the alternate stimulation creates a sweet ache.

He presses against me, the big blunt head of his cock seeking entrance. I take a deep breath, relax, press back against him. There it is. That sweet, intense burst of pain that somehow only serves to excite me more. The head is in, then half the shaft, and in this part of me I can truly feel each millimetre of him as he pushes.

"Is it enough?"

"It is." My heart flutters because he's afraid of hurting me. My own moisture is serving its purpose, though, and all I feel is the pleasure of being unbelievably full. I want to come again. I want to come *with* him this time.

"You feel so fucking good," he says. He always says that when he fucks my ass and I always love to hear it.

I stroke my now tender clit, then give into what I really want. I shove two fingers into my cunt, grind against the heel of my hand. His body weight and frantic movements are bumping me hard against my own palm.

The chaise longue protests as Marc forgets timing and gives over to the feel of me. To the call of his body for release.

"Fuck, Michelle, I'm …"

And I come with him. Hard. I feel him spill into me, filling me with more heat as I come in a long, lazy wave. My body deliciously exhausted and filled.

He settles onto me, kissing the back of my neck, tangling his fingers into my hair.

"Remember how I said all you think about is food?" I ask, flexing my toes warmed from the sun.

"Yeah."

"I lied."

"Pants on fire," he laughs and lays his head down next to mine.

Canadian Postcard
by Lynn Lake

When I decided to take a year off after graduating from high school – to travel across Canada – I thought that the logical place to start would be Newfoundland and Labrador. Now, most Canadians ('foreigners', as some Islanders still call them) think that Newfoundland is just a big, bare, fish-stinky outcropping in the middle of the ocean, but it's actually a lot more than that. The island has forests, lakes, and mountains, and moose, caribou, and other wildlife.

The scenery is spectacular, and the people are really friendly (most of the time I could actually understand what they were saying). I didn't have time to go to Labrador, unfortunately, but I toured all over Newfoundland, visiting places like Gander, Corner Brook, and Stephenville, exploring quaint little fishing villages and outports, kayaking around giant icebergs, and doing some whale- and bird-watching.

I finished off my stay in Canada's most recent province by climbing Signal Hill, and then poking around St John's, the capital. I stayed in a youth hostel on the waterfront, in a tiny, two-bed room. Initially, I had the room all to myself, but on my last night on the Rock, I was suddenly awakened by the sound of the door clicking open, and I saw a girl and guy stumble into the room.

I was lying on my back, watching through half-open eyelids, pretending to be asleep, as they lurched up against the foot of the other bed. I could see them clearly, what with the light coming in through the door they'd neglected to close, and the moonlight through the flimsy curtains. I could smell them even better – Screech, one hundred proof.

'Time to explore the Emerald Isle, Brenda, me lassie,' the guy said, grabbing the girl's humungous tits from behind and squeezing them.

'Jesus, mate!' Brenda blurted. 'I told you I'm bloody English!' Then she moaned softly as her boyfriend kneaded her big boobs, rolled her nipples. 'That's the way, Rodney.'

'Robert,' he said, before spinning her around in his arms so that she was facing him. He pushed the thin straps of her party dress off her shoulders and her naked tits gleamed huge and heavy-looking in the dim light, her nipples swollen obscenely.

Brenda threw her arms around Robert's neck and mashed her lips against his. They kissed and groped each other, right in front of me, Robert running his busy hands all over Brenda's voluptuous body, squeezing her big, round butt, her hands on his butt. Then Brenda slid her tongue in between Robert's lips and they started frenching, slapping their tongues together and swapping spit like there was no tomorrow.

They frenched for what seemed for ever, as I peeped at them in stunned amazement. And then Brenda told Robert to stick out his tongue, which he immediately did, and she closed her lips over the top of it and began sucking up and down on its slippery length, like she was sucking a cock. He groaned and kneaded her plush ass, as she sucked and sucked on his extended tongue.

I suppose I could've coughed or yawned or rolled over, or something – to scare them away – but with my pussy getting wetter and wetter, I didn't want them to stop. Yeah, sure, maybe it was naughty of me to watch, but it's not like I invited them in or anything. So, I held my breath and slid my hand down into my tiny, pink panties, started rubbing my puffed-up clit, gripped my left tit and played with my very erect nipple.

I tried to be as quiet as possible as I felt myself up, but I really needn't have bothered – the two of them were so into each other that only a tidal wave could've dampened their spirits at that point. Eventually, Robert retracted his tongue and cupped Brenda's tits, bent his head down and tongued the girl's nipples.

'Yes!' Brenda shrieked.

Robert's thick, slimy tongue swirled all over and around Brenda's wickedly engorged nips, first one, then the other, over and over, until he finally swallowed one of her buds in his mouth and sucked on it. Brenda riffled her fingers through his hair, Robert's arms shaking a little as he held up her massive tits and pulled on her nipples.

My body flushed with an awesome, overpowering sexual heat, the likes of which I'd never experienced the couple of times that I'd watched my parents go at it. I polished my tingling nub, fondled my super-sensitive tits, and almost came right then and there when Brenda let loose a wail of joy as Robert pushed her porn star boobs together and flapped his tongue back and forth across both of her stiff nipples.

I slowed my hand in my panties – just in time – certain that there was a lot more to come, so to speak. And, sure enough, Brenda broke Robert's embrace and shimmied out of her dress, leaving her as exposed as a dory-bound fisherman in a Nor'easter, except for her high heels. She dropped to her knees and fumbled around with his fly.

'You wanna get a taste of Canada, eh, baby?' Robert quipped, helping her out by unbuckling his pants and pulling them down.

'You know, luv, I really oughtn't to be operating heavy equipment in my condition,' Brenda quipped back, tugging the guy's shorts down and grabbing onto his rigid cock.

Wow! Robert's cock was incredibly long and thick, and Brenda swirled her hand up and down on it like a pro, before encircling the base with her fingers and flicking her tongue across the hood. Robert gasped, as I gasped, and he clawed at Brenda's hair, pulling her face closer, urging her to lick all of his cock. She twirled her tongue all over his bloated dick-tip, then eagerly sucked it into her mouth.

I bit my lip and whimpered, my eyes wide open now, not wanting to miss any of the action. I slid two fingers into my sopping cun, started pumping myself, using my other hand to rub my swollen clit. I watched in awe as Brenda sucked and sucked on Robert's cockhead, slobbered all over his knob, and then popped his hood out of her mouth and started licking his cock like it was a melting popsicle.

She ran her tongue all the way from his balls to his hood, over and over, slurping on his cock with long, slow tongue-strokes. Then she swallowed his hairy balls into her mouth and tugged on his sack for a good, long while. Finally, she disgorged his balls, swallowed up his cockhead again, and then began slowly inching her lips down the shaft of his straining prick. She rapidly inhaled a good three-quarters of the lucky guy's cock, before getting a nice sucking rhythm going, bobbing her head up and down, driving Robert wild, driving me wild.

He soon bleated something about coming, at which point Brenda pulled his dripping dong out of her mouth and stood up, turned around, and bent over and gripped the iron railing at the foot of her bed. She spread her legs and shoved her butt into the air. 'Fuck me!' she hissed.

Robert grabbed her ass with one hand and steered his cock up against her pussy with the other, then slid his prick inside her till he was pressed right up against her bottom. He gripped her waist and started sliding his cock back and forth in her pussy.

I desperately plunged my fingers in and out of my soaking wet cunt, frantically polished my button, my whole body drenched in perspiration. Robert pumped Brenda faster and faster, and I finger-fucked myself faster and faster. He absolutely pounded the brazen Brit's pussy with his cock, as I pounded my mound, the both of us doing Canada proud. His balls smacked up against her quivering bum with each and every frenzied cock-thrust, and Brenda clung to the railing for dear life, her tits flopping all over the place, the bed slamming into the wall. Then her mouth broke open and she let out a low, sustained moan, and stared straight at me as she was blown away by orgasm.

That's when I lost it. I bit my lip until it bled, a truly blistering orgasm churning through my quaking bod, followed by another, and another. I plundered my pussy and buffed my clit, my body wracked with ecstasy. I watched through a salty mist as Robert threw back his head and spurted semen deep into Brenda's pussy, his body jerking with every cum-blast. Then he collapsed on top of her, the three of us totally wasted.

He and Brenda went at it a couple more times that super-hot Newfoundland night, with me scoping out every sensual move. Thank God that the ferry ride to Nova Scotia was six hours long, so I had a chance to catch up on my sleep.

Spanked To Her Senses
by Jim Baker

Alistair Dawson groaned, stretched his arms above his head, and signalled the stewardess for another large Scotch. He caught his wife's disapproving glance from the corner of his eye.

"Yes?" he hissed, glaring at her.

She turned her head away and dropped her book into her lap. He reached over and picked it up, taking a large swig from his drink as he did so.

"*A Critical Review of Religious Art*! Bloody hell! That's what I call jolly reading for the beach. Real holiday stuff!"

Sue snatched the book back, stuffed it into the seat pocket, and stared determinedly out of the window.

Alistair grimaced, took another gulp of Scotch and looked across the aisle at their seventeen-year-old son. Tim stared back at him, expressionless, and then turned his attention back to his magazine.

He picked up his glass and was surprised to find it empty. The stewardess arrived with a refill even as he reached for the call button.

He admired the view of the stewardess's rear as she continued up the aisle, then leaned back and closed his eyes. If all went to plan he would very soon be back in his Canberra apartment with his mistress, Dominique, the French ambassador's P.A.

He smiled to himself at the memory of their last encounter, and felt his cock stiffening.

Dominique had arrived at the apartment in an ankle-length black cape, which she had dropped to the floor as soon as she was inside. She was wearing black fishnet stockings held up by a black garter belt, and nothing else.

She smiled as his gaze moved from her face to her firm, full breasts with their rouged nipples, and then locked on to the thick black bush between her thighs.

"Come here, darling," she said. He walked obediently to her.

She placed a finger, crowned by a long crimson fingernail, on his lips.

"Stand still. Not one sound, Alistair, until I give you permission. Or you will have to be punished. Comprends?"

He nodded wordlessly. She unbuttoned his shirt, pulled it free of his slacks, and tossed it across the room. She kissed him, touched the tip of her tongue to his and raked her long, sharp nails up and down his ribcage.

Alistair gritted his teeth and kept silent. Slowly, she stripped him naked, nibbling at his nipples with her small sharp teeth. She lowered his pants and knelt in front of him, scratching her nails up and down his thighs as she sucked on his balls. Somehow he allowed no sound to escape his lips.

"Très bon. Allons, mon cher."

She stood, took his erection in her hand and led him into the bedroom.

Still standing, she stroked her fingers up and down his

cock until his breath was coming in short, sharp gasps. Then she fixed her dark blue eyes on his, took her hand from the rigid pole of flesh and grasped his balls.

"Now, darling, we shall see," she whispered, and began to squeeze.

Alistair closed his eyes and clenched his teeth until the pain became too great. A deep groan escaped his lips.

"Naughty boy, Alistair. I said no noise, oui?"

She released his balls and stroked his cock gently. The dull ache subsided slowly and her voice whispered in his ear.

"So now you will have to be punished. Come, darling."

She sat on the foot of the bed and he spread himself face down across her knees. The head of his cock pressed hard into the nest of hair between her thighs. She stroked his buttocks.

"So smooth," she murmured.

Alistair tensed for what was to come. He didn't know what she would use to spank him with; they kept a variety of implements beside the bed. He yelped at the first stinging stroke, and knew she was using her favourite, an old, heavy wooden ruler.

The second – much harder – blow brought a shouted obscenity from his lips. Six times the ruler whacked his skin and then he lay, panting for breath, as the pain seared through him.

There was a rustle of movement, and he felt warm liquid trickling on to his stinging flesh. Dominique began massaging oil into his skin. As her hands slid up and down, she moved her thighs back and forth, and the thick forest of hair between them tickled the head of his swollen cock.

Her hands moved lower. A sharp fingernail probed,

133

and he moaned as she slid a long, slippery finger deep inside him. His body writhed, increasing the friction on the head of his cock as she massaged his prostate, until it became too much and, with a huge rasping sigh, he sprayed his hot seed across her thighs, soaking into her pubic hair.

Alistair's smile widened and his cock grew fully erect as he relived the rest of that evening.

He had allowed Dominique to tie his wrists and ankles to the frame of the bed. She played with his cock and tickled his balls until he was rock-hard once more, then reached into a drawer in the bedside table and took out a long, tapered plastic vibrator. She switched it on; Alistair watched, fascinated, as she inserted it deep into her cunt and then withdrew it. The plastic was shiny with her juices.

She switched it off, placed the tip at the entrance to his anus and, twisting it back and forth, inserted the slippery device deep inside him. Then she straddled him, moved up and positioned her cunt directly above his face.

"Now you can taste us both. Eat me, mon cher."

She lowered herself squarely on his mouth, which filled with the taste of her bitter-sweet juices and the saltiness of his own seed.

Alistair began to lick her, sliding his tongue in and out of her cunt and sucking on her pussy lips.

"Up a little, darling. You know where."

Obediently he moved his tongue higher and heard her gasp as he found her clitoris. He flicked his tongue across the hard nub of flesh and she moaned softly. Her body began to writhe as he moved his tongue faster until suddenly she let out a deep groan. Her thighs clamped around his head, and hot liquid gushed into his mouth. For a few seconds her whole weight was on his face, suffocating him, and then she lifted herself up and knelt on the bed beside him.

"Merci, Alistair. Your turn." She reached down between his legs and his body jerked upwards as she switched on the vibrator.

She played with him then, like a cat with a mouse. With her lips and her fingers she took him to the brink, all the time sliding the vibrator slowly in and out, and then clamped her hand around his cock, gripping it savagely to prevent his climax. She held him tightly, watching him with gleaming eyes until his body stopped trembling, and then did the same again.

After the third time Alistair was crying with tears of frustration and she relented, sucking him and running her tongue around the swollen, purple head of his cock. She jacked the base of the shaft with her fingers while she slid the vibrator in and out of his anus with the other hand. Alistair felt himself rushing to orgasm and this time she didn't prevent it. It hit him like an express train and he heard himself bellowing obscenities as jet after jet of hot fluid spurted into her mouth.

Sue Dawson sat next to him, imprisoned by her seat belt. She grimaced as she looked down at the bulge in her husband's pants, well aware that he was lost in an alcohol-fuelled reverie of the mistress he believed to be a secret.

She thought back to the first two years of their marriage and of the fun they'd had together. There had been heady days and nights of art, politics and booze. She was a hippy art student, he an ardent revolutionary, and they were both ready to change the world.

135

Then she became pregnant. Her art became secondary, and Alistair went on to achieve his ambition of becoming someone of importance in the political world. Bringing up Tim had filled her life. Sex with her husband became a routine that was practised very infrequently. Fights and bitter arguments were far more common.

She looked over at her offspring and sighed. Tim was flicking through the pages of an art magazine, probably trying to figure out how he could survive a whole week in the company of his father. He, at least, was sympathetic. He had walked in on her one day recently when she was in tears after yet another row with Alistair.

"Why don't you leave the bastard, Mum?" he said. "You've got plenty of money of your own."

Sue called the stewardess and asked for a large gin and tonic. The holiday was her idea – an effort to bring the family together. She had confronted Alistair on one of the rare days when they had breakfasted together and, surprisingly, he had agreed. His mind had clearly been elsewhere. He had tried to find reasons to get out of it of it ever since, but Sue had remained adamant.

The holiday arrangements were finalised, and then two days later she found out about Alistair's mistress. Alistair and Tim were both away that night. For the first time ever, she went out to a singles bar and got herself picked up.

She lay back, closed her eyes, lost herself in the effect of the gin and the monotonous beat of the engines, and thought back to that crazy night.

She had been very nervous, and it took a couple of stiff drinks at home before she plucked up courage and took a cab to the bar. She was pushing forty and, although she kept herself in good shape, she was surprised and flattered when a good-looking guy of about her own age took an immediate interest in her.

Steve turned out to be a very intelligent and funny guy, far removed from the staid types Sue had been obliged to associate with on the Canberra diplomatic cocktail circuit. After a few drinks, she willingly agreed to go back to his apartment with him.

They sat down on the big settee. The lighting was subdued. Steve had put soft music on and opened a bottle of wine. Sue was still nervous, but he quickly put her mind at rest.

"I'm not sure what you want, Sue," he said. "I think you're a married lady who wants a bit of time away from her husband." He held up a hand to stop her speaking. "It doesn't matter. I've enjoyed this evening very much. If you want to take it further, that's fine with me. In fact it would be very fine with me. If not, that's OK as well. It's your choice. I'd like to see you again, whichever you chose."

Sue closed her eyes, drained her glass, and held out her arms.

"Kiss me."

They kissed for a long time. His tongue played with hers and she groaned deep in her throat as his hand found her breasts. She felt an almost forgotten tingling between her thighs, and ran her hands over his shoulders and down the powerful muscles in his arms.

It was a long time since she'd been in the arms of a really strong man – she smiled to herself at a sudden memory. She had been on a beach with a boy-friend, a body-builder and surfing freak, his name long forgotten. They had been swimming; she was sitting on a blanket and he was lying back on a big smooth rock, soaking up the sun.

"Get us a beer, Sue," he'd called.

"Lazy bastard," she thought. She went to the cold box where the cans of beer floated in a mixture of ice and water. On a sudden impulse she picked up an empty dish from their picnic basket and filled it to the brim with the freezing mixture. She crept back to the rock; his eyes were closed.

"Here, darling," she said sweetly, upended the dish over his crotch – and ran as his scream of shock echoed down the beach. He caught her quickly, threw her over his shoulder and carried her back to the blanket.

"Who's a naughty girl?" he whispered in her ear as he held her easily with one strong arm. She squirmed frantically as he tickled her, and then he put her, face down, across his thighs, rolled down her bikini pants and spanked her bottom. It excited her beyond measure. As soon as he let her go she tore his trunks down and pulled him on top of her for a frantic session of love-making.

She broke off the kiss with Steve and put her lips near his ear.

"Spank me, Steve," she whispered.

He blinked with surprise.

"Do what?"

"Spank me. Put me over your knee, take my panties down and smack my bottom. Hard."

He hesitated for a moment and then chuckled. "You're full of surprises. Are you sure?"

"Very sure."

She was wearing a pair of silk French knickers and she shivered as she felt them slide down over her thighs. He had flipped her over his knees as if she was weightless and pulled her skirt up to her waist. She had lifted herself up a little so that he could take her pants down, and now she pressed down against the hardness

138

between his legs.

For a long moment nothing happened, and then a hard hand smacked her, gently.

"Harder, Steve."

The hand descended again and she laughed. "Come on, big guy. Are you a man or a mouse? Spank me!"

"Okay, sweetheart. You asked for it."

The hand descended again, hard, and this time she yelped, and then again, and again – her arse was on fire and she ground her cunt frantically into his crotch as waves of pleasure racked through her body.

He carried into the bedroom, undressed her, and laid her on the bed. Quickly he stripped off his own clothes and lay down beside her.

She reached down between his legs.

"Christ, Steve," she whispered. "You're massive."

"Just fairly big, baby. Not porn star material."

Sue pushed herself up and looked at what she held in her hand.

"My God," she said. "You're twice the size of ..."

She stopped, confused, and Steve laughed again.

"Your husband? Then he's small, honey. My friend there is bigger than average, I grant you, but not massive. I guess you picked a minnow."

He rolled between her thighs and let the tip of his erection touch the wet flesh between her thighs.

"I'll never get that inside me!"

"Sure you will. Like this, nice and slowly…"

Sue opened her eyes and stretched her arms above her head as she remembered how the walls of her cunt had stretched to accommodate the slow, delicious intrusion of Steve's huge cock. She felt a slickness between her thighs as she relived wrapping her legs around his waist as he thrust into her, bringing her slowly to a glorious, crashing orgasm.

He brought her off five more times that night, with his lips, fingers and cock, and twice more the following morning. He offered to drive her home, but she insisted on calling a taxi, so he kissed her goodbye and gave her a card with his telephone number on it.

"Call me anytime," he said. "I've got a feeling we'll be together again soon."

As she sank into the back of the taxi, her arse stinging, her pussy deliciously sore and her lips swollen from kissing, she began to think about what Tim had said.

Could she find the strength to leave Alistair?

The flight landed in Phuket on time. They walked in silence into the arrival hall, where a Thai man in a dark suit was holding up a board with 'Mr Alistair Dawson' scrawled on it. He handed Alistair a slip of paper.

Alistair scanned it and she saw him smile.

"Sue, darling, I'm so sorry. Message from the boss. Big problem back in Canberra, I'll have to organise flights back straight away."

She strode up to him and stuck her face inches from his.

"I'll bet! Written in French by any chance?"

His eyes widened, then squeezed shut in agony as her knee crashed into his balls. As he crumpled to the floor, Sue went back to Tim, who was watching in amazement. She opened her bag and handed him a roll of dollars.

"Tim. Take the luggage to the hotel, then go out and have fun for a week. Do what you like, be careful, but don't disturb me unless you have to, OK?"

She punched the buttons on her mobile phone.

"Steve? Yes, it's Sue. How do you fancy a week in Phuket...?"

Two Of A Kind
by J. Manx

When I went for the job interview I got a shock. Not a
nasty shock, but the kind of shock you get when you
make an unexpected connection with someone. It rarely
happens. It had never happened to me before, and hasn't
since.

In this case I got a couple of shocks.

I recently got divorced. I used to hold down a good
job in marketing but left work when my daughter was
born. Shortly after, cracks started to appear in my
marriage.

Eventually, I found out my husband was having an
affair. To be honest, I was no longer in love with him. He
left me when my daughter was three and I'd been on my
own ever since. Bit by bit, without realising it, my
confidence melted away. Having been outgoing and
attractive to men I became a rather nervous single mum,
who felt frumpy and wondered whether anyone would
ever find her attractive again.

So, when my daughter was five and started school I
knew I would have to find a job, force myself back into
the workplace and re-build my life.

I'd had about five job interviews – each one
unsuccessful. Interestingly enough, it didn't shatter what

confidence remained. In fact, each failure made me more determined.

Several times I was short-listed for a job but the lack of recent experience let me down.

On the sixth interview my luck changed. It was with a small firm that restored and maintained vintage cars – Jags, Rolls, Bentleys. They also rented them out, chauffeur-driven, for various functions. They were advertising for an assistant marketing director. I'd worked in marketing in the city before and I'd been good. I'd been going places before marriage came along.

I was shown into a small office by a kindly secretary and introduced to the interviewer. That's when the shock came. I felt a flush of excitement, nervousness.

The interviewer was handsome; not conventionally, but his face was rugged, it had lots of character. Something about it made you want to take another look. He introduced himself.

'Hello, Cathy, my name's Paul.'

He smiled – nice smile, but it was his eyes. They crinkled at the sides and lit up. His smile was infectious, made you want to smile back, which I did. What was he? Mid-thirties? Difficult to tell.

He held out a hand.

'If you sit down, we just need to wait until my partner gets here. We'll both be interviewing you.'

He asked me several questions to pass the time – about my journey, where I lived.

Then the second shock. The door opened and in walked a carbon copy of Paul. Paul stood up; noticing my surprise, he smiled.

'Peter, this is Cathy. Cathy this is Peter, my partner and my twin brother.'

I felt a little flustered. I stood, momentarily silent, then gathered my thoughts.

'I'm sorry, I hope you don't think I was rude,' I said, extending my hand, 'you're just so alike … it took me back a little.'

Peter smiled, just like his brother, a confident, amused, sexy smile.

'Don't worry, we get that a lot. It can be quite useful in business.' He winked at me.

The interview was a bit of a blur. I remember laughing, talking a lot, but as is so often the case you come out wishing you'd said so much more. But … I got the job!

After a nervous start my confidence returned and I quickly settled in. I was lucky, working with Peter and Paul was an absolute joy. They were enthusiastic, encouraging and fun. They respected their staff and this was returned with loyalty that was plain to see. It was like working in a large, loving family, everyone looking out for each other.

At the end of three months I got promoted. It was unexpected. We'd been to a meeting with a large company that were interested in using our services to make an early impression on clients. Our plan was to pick the clients up from Heathrow airport, or their hotels, in one of our chauffeur-driven, vintage cars. The client's first contact with the company would give the impression of style and authority. I handled the main part of the presentation. It went well. We got the contract. Peter and Paul were elated. '

It's all been going brilliantly since you joined us, Cathy.'

I began to protest.

'No,' said Paul, 'Peter's right. That's why …' He looked at Paul. Paul nodded. 'That's why we want to promote you to become our marketing director.'

'Really?' I was honestly shocked.

'Yes, really, we don't want to lose you.'

I moved forward and hugged them both. They kissed me on either side of the cheek. I had noticed women looking at these two handsome men and knew what thoughts must cross their minds. I'd enjoyed the same fantasy and as I smelt the fragrance of their musky aftershave the fantasy returned. Things couldn't get much better. We celebrated in a nearby pub. But the celebrations didn't last long. I had to pick my daughter up.

'Listen, Cathy,' said Peter, 'let's celebrate properly. Why not come over to our place at the weekend, we'll make dinner for you and we can really push the boat out?'

I promised that if I could find a babysitter I would love to. I wanted to sound non-committal, not desperately grateful. I had every intention of going, I already had a babysitter in mind.

They lived in a nearby village, in what looked like a three-bedroomed cottage. As the taxi dropped me off, the front door opened and Paul appeared, wearing an apron.

'Wow,' he said, 'you look fantastic.'

Peter appeared behind him, he was also wearing an apron. He gave a low whistle. I began to laugh.

'I hope you've not been fighting in the kitchen.'

' No, it's fine,' said Paul, 'I do the main course, Peter does the sweet, it's all prepared.

We'll eat in about an hour if that's OK?'

'I'm looking forward to it, can't wait,' I said.

They showed me through to a very cosy living room. Peter opened a bottle of champagne and made a toast to my promotion and company success. We chatted for a while and after several glasses of wine I plucked up the courage to become a little personal.

'So, I expected to be able to meet your girlfriends tonight.'

'Oh, we don't have any at the moment,' said Paul.

'Well, I don't suppose that will last very long. Two good-looking men with their own company, you'd be at the top of most girls' lists.'

'Oh, we've not been very successful with long-term relationships, they tend to get a little jealous. Paul and I enjoy the same hobbies. As soon as things start getting a little serious they seem to want to pull us apart, you know have us to themselves exclusive of anyone else.'

'I can't say I blame them,' I laughed.

'Anyway, the thing is,' said Paul, looking at Peter, 'Peter's smitten with you.'

I flushed.

Peter responded. 'Yeah, it's causing a few problems; you see, Paul's also smitten. I'm afraid you've stolen our hearts, Cathy.'

'The real trouble,' I said, bolstered by the wine, 'is that you're both gorgeous.'

They looked at each other, not smiling, but serious. Peter nodded at Paul who got up

and came and sat by me. He held my face in his hands. 'We really are smitten,' he said and kissed me.

My eyes closed. I was aware of Peter sitting down at the other side of me. Paul's kiss was long. When he withdrew he said 'God, Cathy tastes wonderful' and he turned my face towards Peter who began to kiss me. I felt myself melting. I broke away to catch my breath. I felt very aroused.

'I think I'm going to have to try you both out,' I purred.

They looked at each other and laughed. I put a hand around each of their necks and took it in turns to kiss them. I felt their hands, one each, on the inside of my thighs. I hung a leg over each of their laps, easing their access. I could feel fingers pulling my panties aside, then inside. I groaned.

'Oh Paul, she's so juicy'.

I threw my head back.

'Peter, taste her neck, it's so smooth.'

They spoke about me as though they were marvelling over a vintage car, a valuable piece of art or some beautiful animal. I felt slutty, sexy and appreciated. I wanted to be fucked. They pulled down my shoulder straps and eased down my dress, revealing my breasts.

More compliments.

'My God Peter, they're beautiful.'

'Paul, look at those wonderful nipples.'

Fingers still inside me, I felt mouths on each breast, sucking , licking , kissing . One broke away occasionally, to kiss me, before returning to my breast, their fingers still gently working on my pussy. I felt like a spoilt child. I was being spoon-fed sex. They brought me to orgasm and I could see, through partially opened eyes, they were watching me, enjoying my pleasure. I pushed them away.

'Your turn now, boys. Take your clothes off.'

They stood up and I laughed as they eagerly undressed.

Removing my dress and panties, I knelt before them and let out a long sigh.

'Beautiful,' I murmured as their cocks swayed before me. I licked and sucked each one, caressing their bottoms as I did so. After a while, I inserted a forefinger into each pert bottom, gently scraping my nail up and down the soft flesh as I gave them further instructions.

'Now listen boys, I need to spend some time with each of your cocks before I let you fuck me. So Peter, you go and sit over there and watch while I play with Paul and then I'll swap you over.'

I didn't think they were listening as their eyes were closed and they were moaning in response to the ministrations of my fingers. But they both did as they were told. Peter sat in an armchair by Paul's feet while I straddled Paul and lowered my bottom over his mouth. I felt his tongue as he indulged himself. He broke away occasionally to tease Paul.

'My god she tastes fantastic. Cathy, you have the most succulent bottom, the juiciest pussy. I'm sorry Peter, I don't know whether I'm going to be able to tear myself away.' He buried his face back between my legs and I gasped and squirmed with pleasure.

Paul didn't appear to be listening. His eyes were focused intently on me as I licked and sucked his brother's cock. I looked at him wantonly .

'Your brother's very good with his tongue,' I said, 'I hope you can maintain the family standards.'

'God, Peter, you should see what she's doing with her tongue'.

'I can feel it! OOOOOhhhhhh, I can bloody feel it!' shouted Peter.

I laughed. Peter bucked beneath me, gasping as his cock spat pearls of come high into the air.

They changed places. I became further aroused as I felt Paul's impatient tongue licking my pussy and saw Peter's flaccid cock grow as he watched me working on his brother. It wasn't long before Paul came, writhing and groaning beneath me as I held onto his cock, his groans muffled by my pussy which was pressed firmly over his mouth.

147

He sat up, leaned against the sofa and pulled me between his legs. I was sitting, my back lay on his chest and he stroked my hair and shoulders, massaging my nipples and kissing my neck. Paul stood up, now fully erect again. He knelt down, put his hands under my bottom, entered me and began to fuck me. I was in heaven. I crossed my ankles behind Peter's neck and put my arms behind me, around Paul's neck. Paul was massaging my breasts, gently squeezing my nipples. Occasionally, Peter would lean down and suck my breasts and Paul would reach down and massage my clit as his brother pumped in and out. I felt Paul's cock against my back, once more erect. It didn't take long before I reached orgasm again.

Afterwards, Paul took me from behind while Peter watched. By the time Paul had finished, Peter was ready again. I felt as though I was being slowly devoured by two gourmets. I got up and straddled Peter who was sitting on the edge of the sofa. I held his head as he licked my nipples. I eased down and filled up with his cock. I felt Paul's tongue licking my bottom. As I rode up and down on Peter's cock, Paul's tongue followed, the tip dipping and flicking in and out of my bottom. It was sensational.

We had dinner shortly afterwards; I was totally relaxed in their company. I fell asleep later that night in their arms. I felt utterly happy. The next morning I awoke to an empty bed. Paul came in first. We fucked, just the two of us, slow and intimate. The session was briefly interrupted by Peter knocking on the door.

'Come on, you greedy bastard Paul, hurry up, I need Cathy too!'

We both laughed.

'You'd better do as he says, I don't want to be

responsible for any sibling fall-outs.'

When Paul had finished he slipped out of bed.

'I'll go and make breakfast.'

Shortly after he'd gone Peter came in and jumped into bed.

'At last!' he exclaimed. 'All to myself!' and he set to work.

I left the cottage that weekend content and happy to re-live the experience as a treasured memory. I knew I'd never be able to top the sex but it gave me a standard to aim for. I thought of my unhappy marriage, the mistakes of a young woman. That wouldn't be happening again. I owned no one, no one owned me. I was grateful to the twins for showing me what was possible. I had no expectations from them. They had treated me, from the moment I met them, the way a woman should be treated. I determined to make sure I wouldn't be the clingy, jealous character that had put them off other relationships. Besides, I loved my job, it would be silly to jeopardise that for something unattainable.

When I went back to work on the Monday I was professional, upbeat and good-humoured with everyone, including the twins. After several days, Peter and Paul took me to one side.

'Cathy, is everything all right?'

'Of course,' I smiled. 'I couldn't be happier.'

'We just wondered if we'd upset you?'

'No,' I said, 'not at all … Listen, I'm sorry, I didn't mean to come across as stand-offish, that was the furthest thing from my mind. It's just that …well ... it's just that I had a fabulous weekend with you, the best ever, but I don't want you to feel that you owe me anything or that I want anything from you …I don't want you to feel awkward. I love working here, I have no other expectations.'

'Listen, Cathy, you know we're going away on business for a couple of days. Do you mind if we drop in on you on the way back?'

They did drop in, several days later. They met my daughter and got on with her like a house on fire.

'Cathy,' said Peter, 'we might as well come straight out with it; we've fallen in love with you. We both felt it the first time we saw you, and that weekend did it for both of us.'

'Yeah,' added Paul, 'we couldn't stop talking about it, went over and over it. Then, all of a sudden, the solution seemed pretty simple ...'

Peter continued ...

'It may sound a bit unusual but we'd like to share you, we think there's enough love for all of us to be very happy. We promise to make you happy. There, what do you say?'

They both looked like two vulnerable boys waiting to be told they couldn't have a dog for their birthdays. I laughed.

It's the oddest relationship, but it works. Is there an element of cuckoldry? Do they get a voyeuristic pleasure from seeing each other fuck me? Perhaps they like the healthy competition? I haven't quite figured it out. But it works for me. I'm treated like a princess. In the bedroom I can let my imagination run wild. I'm adored, appreciated and fucked voraciously. Sometimes I let them service me individually, other times I indulge myself with the two of them.

We've been living together for six months now. My daughter adores them. I don't think my ex's parents or some of my friends approve of, or accept, the situation.

Tough. Sooner or later everyone will have to accept it

because I've no intention of changing things. Imagine living with a man who is a superb lover, who makes you laugh, treats you like royalty, loves your children, isn't jealous, is masculine, intelligent and sexy. Now, double that. What would you do?

Bathing Minerva
by Jeremy Edwards

I thought Minerva was implicitly sexy even before the Japanese restaurant incident. Though I didn't know her well, I had noticed that she often had a certain sparkle in her eyes, which convinced me that she was a woman who harboured substantial reserves of erotic potential.

I suppose she must have had her eye on me for some time, but I swear I hadn't picked up on it. For one thing, we'd never even flirted. In retrospect, however, it occurs to me that what I had interpreted as a generally-sexy sparkle may have been a specialized sparkle with my name on it. If so, I was oblivious.

Then came the email from Kate, the Comptroller, asking me – and Minerva – to join her for lunch to look over some budget issues. Minerva, who was a close friend of Kate's, tipped me off that the boss had both good taste and a generous expense account; so I was looking forward to this session. And the fact that I was slowly developing a case of the office hots for Minerva – despite my unawareness of anything in the nature of reciprocation – sweetened the pot.

When we arrived for lunch, we looked around with admiration at the downtown Japanese restaurant that Kate had selected for our meeting. Then we claimed our table and made ourselves comfortable – which was not difficult to do in the dining room's soothing environment.

"I didn't even know there was a restaurant on this block," I remarked, after a server had dropped off menus and three glasses of lemon-kissed water.

"This whole building is part of a Japanese hotel chain, actually," Kate explained. "Fairly new in this town, but I'd already heard good things about it."

"Hey, maybe they have those hi-tech toilets with the automatic 'bidet' function," said Minerva, giving Kate a girl-to-girl nudge in the ribs. "Where we can push a button and get our – you know – bathed in warm water."

I knew what she was talking about, having recently learned of these devices from a cousin who could talk about virtually nothing else after a visit she'd made to Japan. But that had been a cousin, giggling her way through a family picnic. This was an alluring co-worker, broaching the topic of intimately sensuous hygiene experiences at a business lunch. My eyes, which had been trained on the rather captivating menu, now glazed over, and I felt a stiffness begin to take shape in my lap.

Kate was laughing, though when I looked up I saw that her face was red and she was giving me a semi-apologetic look.

But it wasn't Kate's face I was interested in. I studied Minerva's face, and I got the impression that her off-the-cuff tidbit of risqué conversation had been performed for my benefit.

Lunch ran its course. And, though Kate would not have liked to hear this, the one and only thing I took away from the meeting was the acute consciousness that Minerva relished the thought of having her pussy bathed by a dedicated stream of automated water, provided by a solicitous plumbing fixture.

I knew it was going to be difficult concentrating on my afternoon work. All I could think about was Minerva jiggling in a hotel bathroom while a jet of hi-tech water kissed her bare underside.

Not surprisingly, this was still on my mind as I rode the subway home that evening. The thought of any woman being that focused on a sensual pleasure between her thighs would have been somewhat arousing to me. For the woman in question to be someone I found sexually compelling to begin with made the situation intensely erogenous.

I had to masturbate before I even phoned her, lest my voice break or I drool into the mouthpiece. As my eyes closed in self-administered release, I saw images of Minerva's face – just her face, with parted lips and merry eyes testifying to luscious sensations below the waist. Water kissing her there. My fingers stroking her. I hadn't come this hard just from masturbating in a long time.

"Minerva? It's Gary."

She laughed sweetly. "I know."

She did? Caller ID ... but I'd never phoned her before, nor had she ever called me. So either she'd programmed my number into her phone just in case, or she'd been expecting me to call tonight based on what had transpired at lunch. I liked each of these theories just fine.

"That was a nice lunch today, wasn't it?" I was trying to be subtle – delicate, even.

Another laugh. "You liked hearing me talk about getting my pussy washed, huh?" Though over the course of several months in the same office Minerva and I had never ventured into sexy banter, it seemed now that once she got started, "subtle" did not appear on her menu – nor was "delicate" in her operative vocabulary. This was obviously a woman who bided her time and then went for

154

broke. No problem. If she wanted to play hardball, I was ready to step up to the plate.

"Yes, I did. Of course, talk only goes so far …"

"You sweetie. Are you offering to buy me an automatic bidet for my birthday?"

"I was thinking of something a bit more old-fashioned."

"As in a bathtub?"

"As in my tongue."

Silence. Had I shocked her? Impossible.

"I'll be right over," she finally said, and the phone went dead. She had my address too, I gathered.

She had a sassy grin on her face when she arrived at my apartment. She squeezed my left hand with both of hers as she entered the room, and the contact made me tingle.

"Welcome," I said, a little awkwardly. "Can I get you something?"

"*Oh,* yeah," she said without missing a beat. "I thought we'd already discussed that."

Hardball. "Fuck, you're sexy," I volunteered.

In an instant, her lips were devouring my mouth and she was squeezing my ass like her life depended on it. She pressed the front of her jeans against my erection in a manner that showed an adroit command of how to simultaneously tease and please, even through two layers of denim.

I was afraid she would make me come just by rubbing herself against me this way, so I pushed my fingers between our groins. As we continued to kiss, I explored the spaces between the buttons on her fly, gently stroking her panties within one or another of the gaps. *Fall into the Gap,* an old commercial said in my head, but with a lewd connotation that Madison Avenue had probably not

155

intended.

"I love your button-front fly," I said in her ear.

"And I love a guy who knows how to use a button-front fly," she replied. "*Oooh* – you're doing the same thing to me that I do to myself through my jeans, under my desk. It's as if I gave you lessons."

The information about what she did under her desk, in the office where we worked together, was almost too much for me to handle at that moment. Added to this was the fact that she had removed one hand from my rear and discovered that I, too, sported a button-front. My cock was going wild as she stroked its edges with the slender finger she'd insinuated.

I took the initiative now to get us out of our respective jeans – which meant, for the moment, getting our hands out of *each other's* jeans. Our shirts, underwear, and socks came off as well – in such a blur that I barely saw Minerva's panties – and soon I was carrying her to my bedroom, her stiff-nippled little breasts pressing into my chest and her fragrant hair grazing my face.

When she was curled up on my sheet with her soft, round behind sticking out in a posture of desire, I had an inspiration. I grabbed something from a bureau drawer. "Be right back," I said as I made a quick dash for the bathroom.

I returned and showed her the silk necktie in my hand. I had saturated it with warm water from the tap, and I rubbed it across the back of her thigh so that she could feel its nurturing texture.

"Would you like me to rub this across you?" I asked, unnecessarily.

"Ohhh," was her simple answer.

To add an additional layer of foreplay to the foreplay, I gently dragged the wet tie across her ass cheeks. Then I kissed the warm, wet streak it had left, while she wriggled her bottom in my face.

"Tell me how good it's going to feel," Minerva said. "Before you do it, just tell me."

"Well," I began. "I'm going to slowly caress your tender pussy with this wet, soft necktie, and it's going to feel very, very good. I can see your slick, pouting lips down there, all ready for the caresses of this silk. I can vividly imagine how this smooth, warm fabric is going to light up every sensor you have in that sweet place between your legs. This necktie, in my hands, is going to make your ass dance with glee."

As if on cue, she gyrated for me. Her left hand grabbed at her clit.

"Yes," I continued, "I expect this is going to feel indescribably good – like your most sensitive, intimate flesh is being bathed in pure pleasure."

"Ohh," she said again, with another delicious wriggle.

"I wouldn't be surprised if it made you …"

"Yes?" she said with urgency.

"Come," I concluded, and I began to make passionate love to her with the specially-prepared tie.

The first thing I noticed, as I held her bottom firm and stroked her slit, was how naturally her own moisture mingled with the liquid that dripped from the tie. Her juice was more viscous than the water, but it flowed freely enough to seep into the fabric, where I knew it would leave stains that I would forever cherish.

Her writhing was slow and sensuous, matching the pace I was setting with the necktie. She rocked from side to side like a little boat on a gentle current, her open sex maintaining contact all the while with the soft tool that pleasured her.

I had pulled the length of tie across her only ten or

twelve times when her ass began to throb in my hand with the first signs of orgasm. Suddenly, Minerva reached down and grabbed the tie from me. She dug it inside herself forcefully, riding the edge of the wet fabric and pulling it across her inner flesh as I'd done, similarly, to her exposed outer lips. Her legs kicked up and down on the mattress and she made short, guttural cries. When she finally clenched her cunt muscles together with a vice-like grip, her entire body was shaking.

My cock, now ready to jump on the bandwagon, bounced upon the back of her thigh. "Grab me," I asked, when her orgasm had subsided.

Minerva not only grabbed me in a delicate, rapturous grip, she treated the head of my cock to a taste of her wet, gaping entrance. Within moments, I was shooting all over her crotch, as she directed my spurts from her clit to her uppermost thigh flesh and back again.

We were satisfied, and we collapsed. She toyed with my long, curly hair.

I was spent but not sleepy. Whereas Minerva, evidently, was sleepy but not entirely spent. No sooner had she dozed off, with a hand cupping her own sex, than I noticed her hips twitching, once every ten seconds or so. Every twitch caused her mound to squeeze against her hand, and her mouth opened a little each time this happened. Eventually, the twitches became even more frequent, until she slipped a dainty finger into her slick cunt, squeezed hard, and had an orgasm in her sleep. She exhaled forcefully, nearly articulating a primal "Oh!" in her dreams. I hugged her, relishing a sensuality that could persist even through slumber.

At that point I, too, must have fallen asleep. The next thing I was aware of was Minerva asking if she could use my shower.

The sound of the water was invigorating, and I started to get hard again as I imagined her bending forward to let the stream rush onto her pussy from behind.

When she was finished, I saw that her use of a towel to "cover herself" was as ineffective as it was unnecessary, my towels not really being of full bath-towel size. As she walked past my bed en route to the pile of clothes in the living room, her ass crack smiled wholeheartedly at me from the generous gap left at her rear. I jumped out of bed and followed her.

I stood by the couch and watched her start to dress, and this time I was able to enjoy the sassy lines of her pink bikini panties around her sleek bottom and fetching mound. Then I remembered something.

"On the phone, I promised to tongue you to orgasm," I reminded her.

"We can save that for after dinner," she said sensibly. She joined me by the couch and touched my elbow. "I have some things I'd like to do to you as well, and I think we're both going to need some calories to make it through the night." Then she swatted me playfully on my still-bare butt and walked back to where her jeans lay clumped on the floor. Without bothering to put them on, she retrieved her phone from a pocket, bending her derrière sweetly my way as she did so.

"Now then … what should we order?" she said brightly, a vision of nipples, tummy, panties … and a face pink with promise.

Darling
by Sommer Marsden

The crowd chanted as the drumbeat of the song began. As one, thousands of people swayed with the opening bass line.

Darling ... darling ... darling!

Ken wrapped Alice in his arms and squeezed her tight.

The crowd crackled with energy. The song was intoxicating. The sky had settled around the throng in the form of pink- and orange-tinted air, casting a look of red velvet on the field.

"Happy Anniversary." His words tickled her ear.

Ten years and they were wrapped around each other like new lovers. Alice's sunburned skin prickled in the cooling night air as Ken's arms cinched her tighter.

"Still my favourite song," she said, arching back to speak directly in his ear. He smelled like warm skin, suntan lotion, and beer.

Darling! The lead singer's voice was a haunting, yearning plea. The crowd responded with a surge of joyous noise.

Bodies brushed them insistently, gently, like bugs bouncing against a screen door in the summer. Every nerve in Alice's body drank in the music, the energy, and the colours. She soaked in the music, the crowd, and the tightly controlled chaos of sounds.

Ten years, and this had always been *their* song. Ten years of good and bad, love and hate, desire and doldrums. Things had not always been easy. They had not always been happy. The time they had considered separating seemed now like a distant memory. A bad dream.

The saxophone bleat carried on the wind, connecting her to him and reminding her of why they were still together.

They were hidden by an oversized Celtic throw, cloaked in cotton, secreted behind its bold patterns. Ken's hands cupped her breasts. He was hard, pressing into the cleft of her ass as he swayed to the song and pulled her along.

She closed her eyes, letting the music and their song fill her senses. The rough voice of the singer brushed her like calloused hands, but Ken moved against her like a second skin – a ghost image of herself. Her hips swayed, charmed by the music and the feel of him.

She remembered the stories her mother had told her of the Indian snake charmers. How they could get the snakes to dance when they played just the right tune. Alice felt like the snake, reptilian and alert, but relaxed. Desire came over her. She should be surprised or even guilty, but she wasn't. Forget decorum. Forget everything else. She slid her hands around to grip Ken's upper thighs and pulled him closer.

My darling ...!

Ken's heartbeat mirrored her own. It thumped strong and steady against her back. The thrum of the bass wound down as Ken's hands dropped to her loose skirt, lifting it. He found the meagre hindrance of her thong and pushed it down. It slid smoothly to the ridge of her knees.

"Take them off." The words plinked in her ears like silver coins into a fountain.

She smiled in the settling dusk. The air had bled from pink to purple.

Alice wiggled her knees, forcing the thong to slip down her calves and puddle around her ankles in the pool of the throw. Everything but their heads was obscured from even the nearest person.

The song stopped, and there was a sudden silence. Ken pulled her so close her breath stuttered in her chest, and his erection prodded her back. Her nipples pushed eagerly against the smooth fabric of her dress.

Would the crowd react? It did at most of the band's shows. REVOLUTION! They were known for their song "Darling". It was legendary – an anthem for their loyal fans.

Encore! Encore! Encore ...! echoed across the huge, grassy field. Fists rose in the air, lighters flickered on like a million fireflies staging a protest. Alice shivered at the palpable electricity in the air. A body brushed her, forcing her even closer to Ken. His cock was eager and hot against her cool skin. He was waiting. Alice knew why.

His mouth found her neck, the spot that made her skin tingle and her cunt turn liquid. His tongue skilfully played against that innocent spot. She moaned. There was something to be said for familiarity.

"All right, people, have it your way!" the lead singer rasped, his voice sounding like a mixture of broken glass and gravel.

The drumbeat started, and the crowd ignited. People danced with abandon. Darkness had fully settled, crouching over the pavilion. The strobes lit up the sky

162

like false lightning skittering across the crowd with a bluish afterglow.

Darling ...!

The soft fabric of her dress rose like a curtain, over her ass, past her hips, and bunched at the back of her waist. Ken's hands pressed against her belly, pulling the fabric taut like a belt.

He didn't have to say anything. Alice bent forward slightly, pushing her ass back against him. His skin was warm and smooth. Her hands danced along his arms, gliding to the fabric of his shorts. His cock was loose, freed from his zipper, but the rest of him was still sheathed in clothing.

One hand dropped to test her. He found her opening and slid a finger in. His cock bobbed appreciatively at finding her so wet. Another finger joined his first, hooking instantly to find her G-spot, and pressing. A wave of warmth and pleasure travelled through her.

She thought of the giggling they had shared while hunting for, and finding, her infamous G-spot. She remembered Ken's impression of a safari explorer: *And now, if we are very still and patient, we may just catch a glimpse of the celebrated and elusive G-spot ...*

Ten years, she thought, feeling her bones turn to rubber. Her pulse quickened as he massaged her deep inside. She felt a secret sadness when he withdrew those marvellous fingers.

My darling ...!

He slid into her, slid in deep and hard, burying into her swiftly. So familiar, yet exciting and new in this setting. Alice sucked in a breath at the first delicious sensation of being entered. She felt his scrotum bouncing against her ass as his rhythm increased. It tickled, but she loved that feeling. His cock was always so strong and sure, thrusting into her, but his balls always seemed so vulnerable, left out somehow. Poor balls. She'd never confessed that thought to Ken. Maybe one day. There were plenty of days to come.

He pulled most of the way out, paused, and then thrust in again. She was almost pinned by his strong arms, but still able to lean forward more, allowing him to go deeper. She relished the audacity of this act. They had never done anything like this. Not in public. Not with a zillion people so near. Her nipples hardened. For all the crowd, they looked like lovers dancing to the music.

The bass became more urgent, the singer nearly screaming to the sky. Ken's speed increased, bending her forward a little more. She was dripping now, her thighs wet from her juices. Bodies, like phantom partners, brushed theirs and heightened Alice's senses. She arched back against his strokes, helping him in deeper, to allow him to push against the softest parts of her. Her cunt gathered around him, tightening to keep him in place. Her orgasm began, a tightening wave in tune with the music.

The rhythm of their sex jammed with the rhythm of the band. They swayed, nearly toppled, but found their balance. All the while, linked cock to cunt, back to front.

Alice felt the tension build in her sex, a tension that was so sweet it was nearly torturous. The friction was maddening as he buried his shaft into her with a greedy grunt. Forgetting her dress, Ken's hands fell to the very tops of her thighs, gripping her hard. His fingertips barely touched the swell of her mound, just enough pressure to be aware of their presence. The possibility of his cupping her there, touching her swollen clit, pushed her closer to orgasm. She waited expectantly and, just when she thought he wouldn't do it, his hands slid forward. One

164

finger slid up her pebble-hard clit to paint her own juices across her engorged skin. Alice gasped, falling into the sensation. The beat of the music centred deep inside her brain.

He pulled her roughly, pounding deep into her as her knees weakened. As always, just before orgasm her legs felt boneless and unstable. Her body bucked. She felt Ken's frenzy and knew he was close.

The bass picked up, and the driving drumbeat battered her ears, the music deluging her senses. The strobes streaked white and blue across the darkness, after-images tattooed on her retinas.

... but life's nothing without you!

They came in one great moment of tension and release. In time with each other. She felt the tickling feeling of him emptying into her shuddering sex. She sighed with each contraction of her cunt, locking him in by clamping her thighs together. Ken's voice was inaudible but tangible by the rush of breath across her ear and cheek. His hands snaked back around her waist, holding her close. He stayed in her. Holding her there as the song wound down again. The crowd was lost in the music. Still jostled and buffeted by the dancing throng, Ken held her and kissed her ear.

Finally he slid from her, leaving her vacant. She didn't retrieve her thong or rearrange her dress. She stayed there in the field and took in the smell of the food vendors, the cheering and singing, the cool grass under her feet. Her husband's sated cock against her skin, and the feel of their combined come between her legs.

My darling ...

The final wail from the singer.

Alice rested her head in against Ken's chest, watching the dark night sky as the next song resonated across the field. She smiled as she swayed. She should be surprised that after all these years they could be so bold. Instead, she was content knowing they still had some surprises left in them, after all.

And maybe, with any luck, they could add another song from the band for the next ten years.

Birthday Blues
by Judith Roycroft

Amber was reaching for the phone when the doorbell rang. It was early for visitors but, as it was her birthday, the caller was most likely her mother. Then she remembered. On Saturday, Nikki Glendenning, her best friend, had whispered to Amber as she was leaving that her present would be delivered on Monday. This was most likely it, Amber decided, walking towards the door.

Through the frosted glass panel she made out the indistinct silhouette of a man. Someone from a courier firm she figured, as she hauled open the door, since the postie had been already. About to greet her caller, Amber's eyes widened and the words stuck in her throat. A mountain of a guy clad in skin-tight jeans, a black bow tie and a white cotton shirt that stretched across his chest and hugged his biceps, stared back at her. Amber swallowed hard. This fine masculine specimen would fit right in amongst a line-up of Chippendales. Certainly impressive and gorgeous enough. And staring at the denim stretched tightly across an enticing bulge was hardly the polite thing to do.

If it's this impressive in resting mode, how generous can it be when aroused?

'Amber Pilbury?'

'Yes?'

'I'm Stephen.' He stepped over the threshold, Amber retreating as he bulldozed his way through. 'Got a stereo? Great,' he said, when she nodded in the direction of the lounge. 'Beats the tinny old thing I carry in my car.' He held up a CD.

Intrigued, Amber stood motionless, observing her unexpected visitor as he took control, deftly slotting the CD in the machine, then pressing the play button. When familiar bump and grind music came filtering out through the speakers, she suspected what was coming next. Glancing up quickly, she met brown eyes, amusement twinkling in their depths.

'I don't think ...really, um, Stephen. It's very good of you, but really, you can't do this in here.'

As though her protests were the expected response, he grinned, and blithely ignored them. 'Happy Birthday from Nikki Glendenning,' he said.

And he began to strip.

Panic racing through her veins, Amber tossed up mentally as to whether she should stop the striptease, or shoot out and bolt the door. Then she decided: to hell with it. It was time to live a little dangerously.

While she stared at the magnificent beast before her, grinding his hips to the beat, he grinned, mischief in his eyes. Her mouth went dry, tongue stuck to the roof of her mouth. Never before had she seen anyone perform a strip-o-gram, which this surely was, as Stephen ripped off his black bow tie, dangled it from one finger and, pelvis thrusting, chucked it towards her. His gaze, black and inviting, never leaving her face as he clutched the front of his pristine shirt and yanked. It burst open, popping buttons, leaving two sleeves, which sat upon his shoulders for a split second before they slipped down his arms and looped about his wrists. He unbuttoned the cuffs and flicked, letting them fall to the floor. His torso, devoid of hair and oiled, showcased his body to magnificent perfection.

Amber's chest tightened; she could hardly breathe as she watched muscles contract as he writhed, charming and seducing her.

Stephen popped the stud button on his jeans, gazing at her through lowered lids. Her heart thumped and a sudden rush of heat pooled between her thighs.

She wanted him.

Badly.

Sexy eyes conveyed an invitation as he touched the tag of his zip, but Amber was rooted to the spot, unable to move forward and assist him. Instead, she stared, watching his bulge swell beneath the heat of her gaze as ever so leisurely, he unzipped his jeans. A splash of kingfisher-blue was revealed between the gaping metal teeth of his zip, as he bumped his hips, emphasising each sensuous movement, ensuring denim slid tantalizingly down those long, satin-smooth legs.

While Amber feasted her eyes on his body, Stephen gave one quick tug of his jeans and they dropped to his ankles. He stood still for several minutes, his bounty in a pouch of blue, while her gaze roved over the coppery body. Like his chest, his oiled legs were nut-brown and hairless and Amber shivered with delight, never before having seen such male perfection. Her throat went dry. She swallowed and stared, beating down a fierce urge to reach out and run her fingers over every glorious bump and hollow in this man's glorious form.

The CD played on, but Stephen stood still. Then, when it became apparent that Amber seemed happy to remain right where she was, doing nothing, he stepped out of his jeans and kicked them aside. He turned his back, which was every bit as beautiful as his gleaming chest.

Amber's gaze slid from the dark brown hair, down his neck and over those powerful shoulders, dipping down to the narrow waist and compact bum encased in minuscule blue briefs.

'Happy birthday, love,' he murmured sexily, glancing over one shoulder at her. 'You can touch. Don't be shy.'

Amber raised her hand to still the pounding pulse in her throat. How could he know that she wanted to touch him? Had he seen the longing in her eyes?

In a daze, she took a step towards him, stopping less than a foot away. The exotic fragrance emanating from his body teased her nostrils, the seductive sway of his hips beckoned for her touch.

It wasn't foolish to want affection from a man. Was it?

She shook her head. *Call it like it is, Amber Pilbury!* Lust. Passion. Good old healthy sex. Those were the emotions she wanted to explore. She sure as hell didn't get any excitement from her prudish husband.

And so she came up behind her strip-o-gram man, slung her arms around his waist and kissed the scented skin. His entire body seemed to stiffen the moment her lips touched his flesh. Stephen exhaled with a long shuddering breath. Emboldened, Amber reached round and found his nipples, and with the tip of her fingers she rolled the hard buds, feeling his spine stiffen against her chest. When she went to draw back, Stephen grabbed her hands and placed them over his nipples again, where she could feel the pounding of his heart. With a sigh he pressed himself back against her.

Amber removed one hand and slid it over his shoulder and down, right down to his waist, his hips, stopping at the band of blue. As her palm slithered over the taut male butt she felt the swift flex of a muscle and an answering throb in her sex. Her thumb crept across to the centre and burrowed beneath the strip of fabric. He groaned as she caressed the crack of his behind, feeling the downy line of hair, rubbing up and along the cleft until he relaxed his buttocks. Taking this as consent, Amber dipped in further, feeling his legs tremble against her, her touch running over his curves and out to caress his naked flank. Amber fell to her knees, left hand clutching the blue briefs, drawing them down with her. Stephen's tormented groan deepened to a harsh growl when she came up to lick one firm globe.

The taste was exotic, salty and male, and she bit, ever so lightly, grazing the sensitive skin with sharp teeth. Beneath her mouth she felt movement as he shuffled his feet apart, opening himself for her. She trailed a finger over the rise of one cheek and then veered inwards, down through the cleft, until she touched the wrinkly sacs.

He cried out, jerking, then bent over, his palms flat on the floor, exposing himself to her.

Amber's eyes opened wide as she marvelled at the sight; he was totally without shame. Excitement shivered through her, and she cupped his scrotum, squeezing lightly, reaching out with a finger to tap the stem of his cock. Heard the stud's quick intake of breath as he sucked air between closed teeth. Identified excitement, an undercurrent of arousal surging out to mingle with her own.

Between her thighs she felt the seep of dew, could smell her arousal.

As she nibbled along the curve of his tight arse, she silently thanked her best friend for such a treasured gift. Amber wished he'd touch her; fleetingly wondered if this

171

were allowed. The strip-o-gram man was here in a private residence, so who would know? Certainly not his employer.

It seemed that Stephen found it difficult to accept her caress without being able to caress in return, for suddenly he straightened, turned to her. Placed his hands on Amber's shoulders and pushed his groin in her face, his hard-muscled thighs bumping into her.

The essence of him, his sexual scent, were potent lures, and Amber took a deep breath before she rubbed her face in his pubic hair.

In an instant his hands went to cradle her head and she felt the pressure of his grip as she began to tongue his cock. It hung heavily out from his thatch, pointing at her, a pearl of moisture on the slit. With the very tip of her tongue she took the pearl into her mouth, tasting the salt of his excitement. Felt him shudder. Then she opened her mouth and surrounded the helmeted head, ringing the base of his shaft with thumb and forefinger, setting a rhythm. Depositing saliva as she tongued him, Amber found it difficult to believe the joy this act was giving her. As she continued to slurp the length of his hot, rigid penis, Stephen released a groan of frustrated lust, grinding his pelvis, a plea for Amber to do more. With the utmost tenderness she cupped his balls, weighing them, caressing them, feeling manly thighs tremble against her.

With her nipples like steel thimbles pushing at the cotton of her bra, her pussy responded, wet and scented in its heat. Clamping her thighs together, applying pressure on her clitoris, Amber flicked her tongue round the rim of his cock. The eye seeped, a never-ending crystal bead forming each time she skimmed it off the top. Now she ached and tingled, her clitoris wanting a touch of its own, and she dropped one hand to finger it. She jerked from her own touch, the tiny shaft too sensitive to endure the lightest of caresses, and reverted to squeezing her thighs together to ease the ache. Opening her mouth, she guided the throbbing penis between her lips and heard the loud guttural sounds of her strip-o-gram man.

'Lady, can I fuck you?'

She leant back, unsheathing his quivering rod, and stared up at him. 'What?'

'Can I fuck you? It's not part of the deal but if the birthday girl is willing, it's OK with my boss. I always carry a rubber, just in case.' Anticipating a favourable response he rifled through his jeans and brandished a packet, already tearing at it with his teeth.

At a loss for words, Amber sat back on her heels, gaping at him. Then she smiled.

'Why not? It is my birthday.'

'Good for you!'

It took him a brief moment to encase his cock in the condom.

With powerful arms he plucked her from the floor, encouraging her to coil her legs round his waist. 'Where's the kitchen?'

She pointed, and he moved swiftly. His erection, impatient, pressing into her. He spied the oak table and ferried her across to it. Once he sat her down, he pushed her back. Gripped her legs and slid her along until they dangled over the end, then flipped her dress up over her head. Yanked at her panties. Cool air caressed her bare skin. When she felt her knickers fall round her ankles she kicked them off, opened her legs for him. Although her sight was blocked with her skirt blinding her, it was as if she could feel the heat from his eyes as they explored every inch. Heard the sharp intake of his breath, the deep inhaling of her scent.

'You have the sweetest snatch. Like the juiciest peach.'

That was the nicest thing anyone had ever said to her during sex, and her eyes prickled with tears of gratitude. 'Thank you.'

Then Stephen's tongue was lapping along her vulva, stopping only while he nibbled on her sex lips, before dipping and stroking the smaller pleats. He suckled the tiny shaft, now and then prodding it with his tongue, Amber thrashing like a woman possessed.

Suddenly his tongue invaded her opening, sending turbulent waves shivering through her.

As Amber's climax racked her body, the spasms imprisoned Stephen's serpentine tongue. His nose stayed buried in her curls, snuffling in the dampness, stimulating her clitoris until she cried out.

He pulled at her skirt, leaving it bunched at her waist and gazed at her, a cute smile on his face. It was torture, waiting for him, her skin buzzing. At last his hands went to touch her; she felt his fingers, busy and sure on the puffy lips, opening her, and a new thrill of anticipation shivered along Amber's spine. Then for a long time he seemed to do nothing but stare, and she visualised the glistening dew, the fragrant nectar, smoothing the way for him. Stephen lowered his face to kiss her intimately, a swift kiss on the small knot before sucking it into his mouth.

She cried out. 'Oh, God. Oh, God. Oh, God!'

Her legs trembled, recognising the desperate need at the heart of her, silently urging her tormentor to suck more fiercely, to take her over the crest of this quivering passion.

When his head lifted she howled in protest, shifting to a sigh when he carefully eased two fingers into her. The morning sunlight streamed into the kitchen and fell across his skin so that it shone glossy, like copper, the rise and fall of his muscles an exhilarating action as he pumped his fingers in and out of her tunnel. With grunts and moans Amber conveyed the intensity of her pleasure, as he plundered harder, faster, while her head thrashed on polished timber, cushioned by her cap of hair.

'Please!' she begged, when the stud removed his fingers. 'Please. Don't stop!'

With both hands Stephen grasped her thighs and moved in so he was flush with the edge, then she felt his rod nosing in, searching out the hot, vulnerable core of Vesuvius. He began to move back and forth, his fingers gripping her hips, holding her in place.

Amber gritted her teeth, a crescendo of excitement building deep inside her as he held her steady, grinding into her, sparking sensation after exhilarating sensation, in her pussy. In her legs. In every fibre of her being.

Warm masculine fingers slipped between bodies, his thumb urging her clitoris in tight, sensual circles. Amber responded fiercely, lifting her backside off the table and thrusting her pelvis, urging for more pressure on the tight nodule, the nucleus of her pleasure. As the tingles began to build, brewing vibrations, Amber's pleasure crested, and then a cry like a wild creature erupted from her throat and she was lost in the maelstrom of sensations gripping her flesh.

Stephen rammed his cock into her, embedded to the hilt. Drawing on the shuddering convulsions that stemmed deep within her, he cried out, hard thighs shaking against the curves of her buttocks, his spasms fierce and powerful, wringing every drop of pleasure

175

from her.

When they were calm, locked together, with only the sound of shallow breathing joining the muted ticking of the kitchen clock, Amber opened her eyes and looked at her gift from Nikki. Perspiration coated his torso, a sheen that glossed his bronze skin as his chest heaved in the brilliant morning light. His penis shrivelled and slipped out of her, and he stepped back.

Propping herself up on her elbows, Amber watched him walk away, drawing in her breath as she observed the play of powerful muscles, and ran her gaze up to look once more upon the most perfect butt in God's illustrious creation.

By the time she followed him into the lounge, he was pulling on his jeans. He grinned at her as he zipped up and snapped the stud in place. Her eyes surveyed the taut stomach, his smooth chest.

She just had to ask.

'What do you do, besides this? If you don't mind my asking,' Amber added hastily, as she caught his wry grin.

'Would you believe I'm putting myself through University?'

'It seems everyone I meet these days is doing just that. What I'm really asking is how you got that delicious bod?'

Stephen laughed. 'Lugging barrow loads of bricks on construction sites. Hefting timber. Better than going to the gym. I get paid for working out. And this extra little job is my playtime. It gives me plenty of perks. ' He grinned, bent and picked up his discarded shirt.

As she watched him slip it on, Amber was amazed how it all came together after the way he'd ripped it off. Apparently it was especially made for rough treatment.

'Sorry, but I have to get going,' he said, walking over

to remove his CD. When he turned back he stood gazing at her. Then he approached, reached out and stroked her cheek. He kissed her. Not hot and hungry, like before. Soft and sweet. 'It was a pleasure, Amber Pilbury.'

Would she ever see him again? The urge to ask was strong, but she played it cool and held her tongue. As much as she enjoyed the erotic interlude, to Stephen it was a matter of business. He had been paid to strip. Heat flooded her face as her mind took the next step. Paid to pleasure her? In the pit of her stomach, she felt ill. Paid sex? Had she plummeted so low? The least she could do was thank him. But to her horror, what came out of her mouth, she should have kept to herself.

'Will I see you again?' Disgusted with her wayward tongue, Amber clapped her hand over her mouth, and she waited for him to rubbish the idea, to tell her that this was a one-off, paid for by her friend, Nikki Glendenning.

He took another step towards her and cradled her face in his hands; let her down gently. 'If you want another strip-o-gram.'

The heat in her cheeks scorched like an open flame. To think that the intense pleasure she experienced with Stephen, the enjoyment he, too, received, meant nothing more to him than a paid performance. Her hands clenched at her sides as she wondered what redeeming words she could say. 'Thank you, Stephen. It …it was a lovely present.'

'No, Amber. Believe me, it was a present to me,' he said chivalrously. He kissed the tip of her nose, then lightly brushed his thumb back and forth across one cheek. 'You're a lovely young lady. Your husband is a lucky fellow.' His lips were soft, achingly tender, scented with her pussy, as he touched them to her mouth.

A tsunami of regret rose in her and she blinked rapidly

177

to hold back the unwanted tears; why was she stuck with a husband as unfeeling as Derek, when she deserved someone as affectionate as Stephen?

Oh yes! She deserved someone like Stephen. And she couldn't wait for her next birthday to come round. But...

Who said you couldn't celebrate your birthday every day of the week?

Railway Signals
by J. Manx

A new job. That, I was excited about. But the company was located in the city. I lived in the suburbs. It meant commuting, and that I wasn't looking forward to. I bought a weekly ticket, and on Monday morning stood on a crowded platform waiting for the 08.12 to Charing Cross. The day was stressful. The usual mix of people; some friendly, some not; some helpful, some indifferent. When I got home, absolutely knackered, I spent a good part of the evening moaning to my husband, mainly about the train journey.

The next day my feet were aching, no doubt from having to stand during the previous train journey. I stood on the platform, figuring out whether I would be able to endure years or even weeks of commuting. The train pulled in. Passengers crowded round the doors and then piled on. I hung back. I'd be damned if I was going to behave like a yob, even if it meant waiting for the next train. It was packed, standing-room only, but there was room for me, a last sardine. As I moved to the door a man, mid- to late-thirties, stood aside. He looked at me and smiled. It was unexpected so I smiled back then got on the train. He had nice eyes.

Another bloody crap journey. To make it worse, some

bastard farted.

That evening my husband got another earful.

'Why don't you get an earlier train?' he said, from behind a paper, 'it'll add another hour or so onto your day but I bet it'll reduce the stress.'

Made sense. The next day I caught the 07:20 and got a seat. As I settled into it, I noticed the man opposite and recognised him from the previous day. He was the one who let me get on the train. We nodded politely to each other. He looked clean and smart. He was handsome.

'You've lightened up a bit, journey better?' said my husband that evening. I was in a better mood.

'What a difference it made getting a seat; my feet have stopped aching, perhaps I can start wearing some decent shoes.'

The next day, Handsome Man was again sitting opposite me. He smiled and nodded; I smiled back. Neither of us had a newspaper and it was difficult, sitting opposite each other, not to make occasional eye contact. When it happened it was brief, momentary. When he appeared to be looking out of the window I was able to settle my eyes on him. He was clean-cut, short hair, a bit of grey, strong face. Good suit, polished shoes, athletic-looking, ex-Army officer? accountant? banker? He was wearing a wedding ring. He turned his face towards me and I looked away.

That weekend I had my hair done. Whilst getting it dried I relaxed and thought of Handsome Man. I don't know why. He was back in my head. Later, when I was shopping for clothes, I had a vision of him complimenting me on a skirt I was thinking of buying.

There I was, sitting on the train, with him opposite and he said, in front of everyone else, 'you look nice.'

The weekend went and Monday came, too quickly. When I sat on the train, I felt a figure sit heavily beside me. I turned to see Handsome Man.

'I do apologise,' he said, 'I almost tripped.' His voice was smooth and velvety. I smiled. 'That's OK.'

I really enjoyed the journey. Normally, one feels a little awkward sitting closely, next to a stranger. There's a heightened sensitivity to any contact and by the time you disembark you're already stressed by the physical effort of keeping oneself to oneself. At first, I was consciously aware of keeping my leg from touching Handsome Man's. So, I think, was he. But, bit by bit, I relaxed the tension in my leg and it rested neatly against his. I sat, feeling strangely excited. I could feel his hard shoulder pressed into mine. He smelt of fresh citrus aftershave. I wanted to rest my head on his shoulder. When we pulled into Charing Cross he got up, opened the door, and let me out first.

'Thank you,' I said, staring right into his eyes.

'Pleasure,' he said and smiled back. The next day Handsome Man didn't seem to be on the train. I felt a little disappointed. When I got home from work that night I had a shower then lay on the bed reading. Handsome Man entered my head again and I began to fantasize about him making love to me in a plush hotel room. Then my husband came in and caught me masturbating. 'What's all this, then?' he laughed. I was very irritated at having the fantasy interrupted, but pleased that his cock could finish me off.

The next two days I was disappointed. I didn't see Handsome Man. He wasn't on the train. I'd worn a new outfit and was hoping to see him. I felt elated when I saw him on the third day, standing on the platform. I moved near him and stood behind him. When he got on the train I followed and sat opposite. As we settled, he looked across and smiled. The train moved off. We caught each other's eyes several times, smiled, then looked away. Then the strangest thing happened. After several stops, we caught each other's eyes again. This time we didn't look away. We just stared across the carriage at each other, just stared into each other's eyes. I felt perfectly relaxed looking into those deep grey eyes. We didn't smile, we just stared, fixated, concentrated, trance-like. I only broke the state when I became aware that the train was slowing down as it reached Charing Cross. I noticed Handsome Man looking at my legs as I uncrossed them, whilst preparing to disembark.

The next morning I put stockings and higher heels on. My husband came in as I was putting my skirt on.

'Wahaaay,' he said, irritatingly. 'Must be my birthday. I can't remember the last time I saw you in stockings, what's the occasion?'

'No occasion, just a stifling train and no air conditioning at work. It's very uncomfortable wearing tights.'

He ran his hand up and down my leg, then pulled me towards him.

'How about a quick one, to set you up for work?'

'Sorry darling, I don't want to miss the train.'

I felt a little guilty but very excited. I drove to the station and parked the car. Before I got out, I undid several of the lowest buttons on the side of my skirt. I sat opposite Handsome Man. He smiled at me and I smiled back, demurely, then slowly crossed my legs. His smile disappeared as his eyes fixed on my exposed thigh. The man next to him was also looking but I was only concerned with Handsome Man. I'd bought a book which I pretended to read. Occasionally, I would shift a little in my seat, adjust my thigh and point the toes on my crossed leg a little. I looked up from my book every so often and fixed Handsome Man with a brief, inquisitive stare. The man next to him had his mouth slightly open and looked as if he was about to dribble. He was looking at me furtively and he eventually re-positioned his newspaper so that he could stare over the top at my thigh whilst still appearing to be reading. Handsome Man glanced sideways at him and then raised his eyebrows at me. It was the sexiest train journey yet. When I got off I felt Handsome Man's eyes following me down the platform. I sashayed, just a little.

The following day was better still. Handsome Man followed me onto the train and almost pushed a fellow passenger out of the way so that he could sit beside me. I'd worn stockings again, with the same skirt and heels, in the hope that I could reproduce the previous day's performance. As the train pulled off I opened my book, crossed my legs and felt my suspender tighten and dig into the thin suit material covering Handsome Man's thigh. His trousers were made of soft, expensive cotton and they had a sharp crease in them. He'd bought a large newspaper, *The Telegraph*, which he spread out, holding it so that it partly covered my thigh. I carried on reading my book and relaxed so that my body settled against his. I was aided by the movement of the train. As we wobbled along the tracks I was given the excuse to brush the side of my head against his suit jacket so that my hair caressed his shoulder. I had rested my elbow, very lightly, on his thigh. When the train jerked slightly I would apply pressure, pushing my elbow and part of my forearm against his leg. I found it intensely exciting. At one point Handsome Man turned his head above mine and I felt his nose briefly nestle in my hair, gently inhaling the fragrance of my perfume. He exhaled, his warm breath spreading the aroma of his citrus aftershave. I was highly aroused and squeezed my thighs together, attempting to stimulate myself further, but I couldn't position myself properly. I felt frustrated, but wonderfully so.

The journey had become the highpoint of my day. I bought clothes with Handsome Man in mind. I knew I had good legs; they looked fantastic in heels. I was forever being complimented at work, but all my efforts were for Handsome Man. I'd bought new, expensive bras and different shades of stockings, I wore garters, split skirts, unbuttoned blouses, painted nails, carefully applied make-up. Don't get me wrong; this was all done in an understated way. To see me on the train, I looked smart, sophisticated and desirable. But the raunchier clothing underneath made me feel like a wanton slut. I wanted Handsome Man to believe that beneath that smart exterior was a passionate vixen who would pamper his cock, smother him with juicy pussy, be ridden like a beast, who was a beast.

I felt a great sense of disappointment if we missed each other or ended up in different parts of the train. It put me in a flat mood all day. When this did happen, a subsequent shared journey became even more sexually charged. The most exciting part of the journey was when the train pulled into the station. Handsome Man would stand behind me and put his hand on my shoulder or thigh or, God it only happened once, my bottom. Just for a second or two, whilst everyone else was putting papers away or getting coats or bags from the racks. No one would see, but I would feel a kind of shock as his hand settled on me. Once, he rested one hand on my thigh, and I knew he could feel my suspender, and one hand on my bottom. It was brief but exquisite. He let out a quiet, almost painful sigh, and I felt his breath on my hair and the back of my neck. When I got to work I had to go straight to the Ladies where I stood, leaning against a wall, trembling in a cubicle, my hand between my legs.

So, things went along like this for some time. Fleeting touches, flirtatious looks, occasional words spoken, but no more than 'hello,' 'excuse me' or 'thank you'. Neither of us needed words. It was just those three senses, sight, touch and smell that were employed to take me to a level of arousal I hadn't experienced before. I didn't want to fuck Handsome Man but I did want to touch him, to tease him, to arouse him.

I would have been quite happy for the situation to remain as it was.

One morning, the usual feeling of anticipation was replaced with one of resignation when, with no sign of Handsome Man, the train pulled in, two carriages short and already looking almost full. There was an announcement that the train would be going straight to Charing Cross, so I decided that, rather than wait for the next one, which was just as likely to be full, I might as well join the rest of the cattle on the truck. As the train slowed to a halt, I bustled up to the carriage along with the other passengers and just managed to squeeze on, a little worried that I would fall out before the doors closed. Just as the doors were about to close, Handsome Man appeared and squeezed on beside me. I smelt that reassuring freshness of citrus aftershave.

We were bunched so tightly there was minimal room to move. I had my back to the doors, squeezed into a corner. Handsome Man turned to face me and at the same time reached up to grab hold of a rail and steady himself. His coat, which was open, spread like a cape, surrounding me, and concealing me from the view of the other passengers. Our bodies were so close that as the train skimmed along the tracks the gentle swaying caused our bodies to connect, detach and re-connect. I'd never been this close to him. The smell of his aftershave was tantalizing. His chin was over my head. I looked up, he looked down and we smiled at each other. We moved a fraction closer, enough to ensure unbroken contact. I pressed my breasts into him then I felt his free hand on my bottom. He caressed it in circular motions slowly, lightly. He then moved his hand to the side of my thigh, pausing over my suspender before rubbing his thumb back and forth along it. I rested my forehead on his chest and closed my eyes to enjoy the feel of his hand on my thigh. After a few minutes he moved his hand and ran it gently up and down my back. I felt his breath on the top of my head and felt his nose touching my hair. His hand now moved to my front and began to caress my breast. All his touches were light and slow, there was no urgency. Having felt my nipple harden beneath the shirt his hand moved to my shirt buttons. I had left the top three undone hoping to titillate, never dreaming we would be this close. He began to undo the buttons and, for a fleeting moment, I was tempted to remove his hand, stop this from going any further, but curiosity and arousal doused that temptation and I let him continue. He undid a further two buttons and slipped his hand inside my blouse. He caressed my breast through the lacy bra I was wearing and then moved his hand up to my shoulder and slipped off my bra strap before moving his hand back down and easing my breast from its lacy cup. His hand was smooth and dry. My nipple was hard and erect. I buried my head deeper into his chest, my mouth pressed against the soft cotton of his shirt as I tried to stifle a groan. I felt my nipple being rolled and massaged between his thumb and forefinger. Intense pulses of pleasure flowed from my breast to my pussy. I felt my legs almost buckle and put a hand on his chest to steady myself. It was the overcrowded, noisy, dirty, 07:20 to Charing Cross and I was in heaven.

I put my hand on his crotch and could feel his hardness. I undid his fly, put my hand in his trousers and gently worked his cock free. It was warm and thick and smooth. I ran my fingers along it, exploring the length and shape. His breathing became heavier and deeper, his breath warm on my head. And, although excited, he maintained a steady pressure on my nipple which was still sending out waves of pleasure. I gripped his cock firmly, by the head, and began a steady movement backwards and forwards. I was surprised when, after several strokes, I felt his hand tighten on my breast and felt the warmth of his semen ejaculating onto my hand and wrist. As he came, his head drooped and I heard gentle groans, a few seconds of silence then a whispered 'thank you'. I held his cock, feeling it slowly deflate, and put it back in his trousers before it grew erect again. I spent the short remainder of the journey nestled against his chest, still concealed by his open coat. When the train stopped, just before I got off, he said, '07.20 tomorrow?'

I nodded, got off the train and walked towards the exit, still excited by the feel of his semen on my hand.

That weekend I bought a season ticket.

Also available from Xcite Books

20 bottom-tingling stories to make your buttocks blush!
Miranda Forbes has chosen only the finest and sauciest tales
in compiling this sumptuous book of naughty treats!
Spanking has never been so popular. Find out why ...

ISBN 9781906125837   price £7.99

The True Confessions of a London Spank Daddy

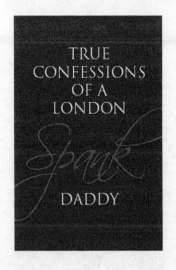

My name is Peter, I'm 55 and I'm a Spank Daddy. I offer a spanking and disciplining service to women...

Discover an underworld of sex, spanking and submission. A world where high-powered executives and cuddly mums go to be spanked, caned and disciplined.

In this powerful and compelling book Peter reveals how his fetish was kindled by corporal punishment while still at school. How he struggled to contain it until, eventually, he discovered he was far from alone in London's vibrant, active sex scene.

What he learnt on the scene helped him to understand the psychology of women who wanted to submit to submissive discipline. Many were professional women, often juggling a demanding job and family. They needed to occasionally relinquish all control, to submit totally to the will of another. Others sought a father figure who could offer them the firm security they remembered from their childhood when Daddy had been very much in control.

Chapter by chapter he reveals his clients' stories as he turns their fantasies into reality. The writing is powerful, the stories graphic and compelling.

Discover an unknown world...

ISBN 9781906373313   Price £9.99

NEW!!

Ultimate Curves for gorgeous,
Sexy, lovable, ladies…

Free stories, dating
and plus-size lingerie

www.ultimatecurves.com

NEW! XCITE DATING

Xcite Dating is an online dating and friend-finder service. With Xcite Dating you can meet new friends, find romance and seek out that special person who shares your fantasies.

Xcite dating is a safe and completely anonymous service. Sign-up today – life's too short not to!

www.xcitedating.com

For more information about Xcite Books
please visit

www.xcitebooks.com

Thank you!

Love, Miranda xx